No Going Back

No Going Back

An Erotic Novella

Emily Richards

Swanky Post Publishing

Swanky Post Publishing is a division of Falling Rock
Entertainment, LLC.

Published by Swanky Post Publishing, Seal Beach, CA
www.swankypost.com

ISBN-10:0692803440
ISBN-13: 978-0692803448
Library of Congress Control Number: 2016918438
Falling Rock Entertainment, LLC, Seal Beach, CA

Cover art and design: Roberto Antonio Martinez

We keep moving forward, opening new doors, and doing new things,

because we're curious, and curiosity keeps leading us down new paths.

—Walt Disney

When the winds of changes shift,

May your heart always be joyful.

—Bob Dylan

Dreams

Dreams, the ones we remember, are often scary, so scary we struggle to wake ourselves or scream only to find there is some invisible force preventing any sound from escaping and other times our dreams are a mish-mash of images and scenes amusing, and occasionally erotic.

One of my friends, Jackie, keeps a pen and paper by her bedside so that when she wakes up—either in the middle of the night or first thing in the morning—she can scribble down her dreams or at least what she can remember. Dreams are so elusive, like trying to hold onto water—they slip right through the grasp of our consciousness.

The weird thing about recurring dreams is that we have a sense when they are about to come onto the big screen in our sleep. I have two recurring dreams. One is about flying as a passenger in an airplane. Either landing or taking off, the plane has some mechanical problem, and it seems as if we are about to crash, flying through a city, between buildings, under telephone and electrical wires. The cities are always different, and I am never with anyone I know on the flight. We never crash in my dream—just tons of anxiety.

Another dream is about a house with multiple levels, and once I enter the edifice, I think, *Oh no, here we go again*. In this dream, I can't go back—only forward, and to move forward I must venture down to lower levels. Descending each level is frighteningly dreadful and inhabited by some kind of evil spirit or being. The only way to get out of the house is to go through all the bottom levels and then the top levels. The disturbing thing about the well-lit upper floors and rooms is that they are eerier than the dark and ghoulish lower levels.

Then something strange happens in this dream, as often happens in dreams. I start to get aroused when I am on an upper level. I know I must enter one of the rooms. I enter the room through an nondescript door. Once inside the room, I must pass through a white veil into an inner chamber. Everything in the inner room is white, and inside this room is a bed with a gold post on each corner. Next thing I know, I am bent over the end of the bed, lying facedown. My wrists and ankles are restrained by a chord to each of the gold posts. I am blindfolded by a white silk sash. I am wearing a conservative church dress, sometimes white and other times a floral print. The room is still and silent. The only sounds I can hear are the beating of my heart and my breathing.

The beating of my heart starts off as a deep murmur but builds to a pounding equal to a bass drum.

I hear the mechanical engagement of the lock on the door, like the one you might hear in a hotel room when you enter the keycard into the sensor slot. I listen to the doorknob twist open. A gust of wind blows, and I can hear the veil swishing against the white silk comforter. The door closes. I listen for footsteps. There are none.

My heart races, and I am aroused—so aroused that I am getting wet. I can sense someone has passed through the veil and is standing behind me. I want to say something—scream, fight against my restraints—but I do nothing. I want him. I want him to take me.

I can feel him lift my dress over my hips. His fingers check me for my wetness; satisfied, he enters me. I quiver, my legs quaking as he slides in and out of me, filling me. Now pounding faster, he seems to grow inside of me. He tenses and then releases, and I know I have pleased him. I feel something warm and beautiful inside of me; then this warm fluid leaks out of me onto my thigh.

And just as quickly as he mounted me, he is gone, and I am free of my restraints and free to leave the building. I walk out into a beautiful open field on a glorious bright sunny day. The sky is a pale blue and cloudless and a cool breeze refreshes my body. I pause and think of looking back, but I never do.

Winds of Change

Late in the spring of 1998, on a breezy, sunbaked afternoon in a small village in Central America, the proverbial winds of change not only shifted but also brought along their offspring, the seeds of change. I suppose all of us can look back on pivotal moments in life when we reach a crossroads filled with seemingly obvious choices. Yet we are hijacked by unintended consequences, which seem to alter our personal history drastically. Other times we plod though our day unaware that we passed through a crossroads at all.

Some people may say, "Well, I didn't choose to get into this accident that caused irreparable damage to my body"—or some other misfortune. While that is somewhat true, any event is still an unintended consequence of a myriad of choices putting you in that exact place at that exact time. For example, what if you get into a car accident on your way to work? Just think: if you had popped right out of bed instead of hitting the snooze button or had slept in a few minutes longer, obviously you wouldn't have been at the place of the accident at that exact moment. Then think of all the choices you made between waking up and having the accident. Not to mention the time you decided to go to bed, which would inevitably influence the time you woke up.

I remember a time when a man dropped off his wife at Los Angeles International Airport. The airport was doing some major construction at the time, some of which included the use of large cranes. It just so happened that after he dropped off his wife, and he was moving toward the exit, one of these massive cranes broke and fell right on his car, killing him instantly. I recall thinking if he had kissed his wife and held her a moment longer, he would not have been in that exact spot at that exact time.

Unknown to my husband, William, and me, this was one of those times, although our experience did not involve an accident or a death. It was more akin to Copernicus disproving the geocentric universe.

It started off innocently enough, with William receiving a grant from Brigham Young University and the Foundation for Ancient Research and Mormon Studies (FARMS) to write a book on the lands and peoples featured in the Book of Mormon. William had spent a great deal of his life studying the Book of Mormon, not only from a

3

spiritual perspective but also from a historical perspective. We were taught, as members of the church, that the Book of Mormon was a literal history of the peoples who populated the Americas and the most accurate book ever written. The exact locations of these people remained a mystery. William believed he had a good idea of the locations, in Central America, of the lands mentioned in the Book of Mormon, and more importantly, he wanted to bring the book to life for students and members of the church.

William asked if I wanted to go with him, adding that we could spend a few days in Cancun on our way back. Really? A chance to hike through the jungles of Central America with my husband and then spend a few sun-soaked days on the pristine beaches of Cancun? It took me all of a nanosecond to say yes. I think I spent the next few days bouncing around the house with Tigger-esque enthusiasm.

Having been an athlete all my life, including playing on the women's basketball team at BYU, I was more of a guy's girl. I liked to camp, hike, fish, and hunt. I loved adventure, yet when called upon, I could spin on a dime and get all dolled up and look pretty good. I was five foot nine and blessed with an athletic body that was still in pretty good shape. Although I still had to work at it, I had to admit that I could look attractive when I wanted to.

As a wife and mother of five—Jessica, Hannah, Connor, Luke, and Miranda—my life was definitely about moving forward, experiencing new adventures, and making new discoveries. Getting the household organized before our trip would take Martha Stewart–like execution, which was one of my fortes. Also, fortunately, my parents were retired and close enough to be the "adults in the home," as they preferred to call it, but they were actually the babysitters. As you might have guessed by now, William and I were both Mormon. We were both born into the church and came from an esteemed Mormon pioneer heritage.

William and I had graduated at the top of our class from BYU and then BYU Law School. William was a very respected and successful lawyer by just about any standard. I put *respected* first because being respected and trusted by your clients and peers was always something paramount to both of us.

We put off having children for a few years after we got married. Once we decided the time was right, they arrived on schedule. We eventually moved to Pacific Palisades, a suburb of Los Angeles. I had decided to put my law career aside to raise the children, and I loved

4

it—no regrets.

When the kids were little and napping, I experimented with writing children's books, exclusively for my kids. This habit of writing led to other works and other areas of interest, including helping William with research projects. I found, after taking a few courses at the University of California, Los Angeles, and working with a strict editor, that I had a knack for writing. I loved history and was profoundly curious about a quote attributed to Robert the Bruce: "History is written by those who have hanged heroes." In other words, by the winners. A simple example: had the British quelled the American Revolution, Benedict Arnold would have been hailed a hero, and the Founding Fathers—George Washington, Thomas Jefferson, Benjamin Franklin, and many others—would have been hanged as traitors. My love of history and of writing eventually led to a couple of well-received published historical novels.

William is an excellent provider, friend, lover, and father. After twenty years of a wonderful marriage and family life, everything was moving along without any real glitches. Everything seemed to be happening right on schedule. The kids were growing and always seemed to have something going on, either with school, church, or sports. Jessica, Hannah, Connor, and Luke had inherited our athleticism and were always playing sports in their free time. They were so competitive that I often felt like a referee in a boxing match. Miranda, our youngest and our diva, avoided sports like the plague, even though she was our most athletic child. She was into anything and everything dramatic. She loved the spotlight and the stage and would use any kitchen utensil she could get her hands on as a microphone. Life was just really great.

Between the two of us, church-wise, William had always been the more devoted. Not that I was a wayward soul, but he just paid more attention to the details, scripture study, prayer, reading, and learning. It was his thirst for knowledge that helped drive his religious zeal.

5

Seeds of Change

It was in the remote village of Lacandón in Central America that a door opened, and the winds of change blew right through and forever altered our lives. William's pit-bull-like grip on wanting to know the facts triggered a domino effect. It was like peeling back an onion, one layer at a time.

"Are you seeing what I'm seeing?" William asked.

"Yes," I said confidently.

"Are you thinking what I'm thinking?" he asked again, while his eyes followed a dark-skinned man and woman dressed in their white tunics, natives from this village, walking in front of us.

"I think so," I answered not so confidently as I looked at the short, dark-skinned couple with almond-shaped eyes.

"Good. I don't want to influence your observations with my own, so take notes, and we'll compare when we get back to our hotel."

"I feel like we're somewhere in Asia, but shouldn't this feel like the Middle East?" I murmured.

Later in the evening, after getting back from the village and visiting the Lacandón people, we decided we would shower in our hotel room, eat dinner at the hotel restaurant, and then relax in the hot tub. I was standing naked in the bathroom, my hands tracing over my athletic yet feminine body. With the help of exercise and good genetics, I had held up pretty well. There were areas exposed to the sun that were not covered in dirt and grime; the sun-kissed pinkish tones reminded me to cover up. Plenty of sunscreen was what my snow-white body required for any extended time in the sun.

I felt a sense of arousal as my hands traced over my body. I opened the door to the bathroom, peeking my head out through the steamy mist. "Do you want to join me in the shower?" I asked.

A little startled, William looked up from his notes. "Yes!" he said, jumping up at roughly the speed of light and undressing all in one motion.

The warm water cascaded down my body as William's hands worked soap into my skin. He reached around and began washing my belly and then moved up to my breasts. He pressed against me and kissed the nape of my neck, sending chills through my body. I pressed my butt against his bulging erection. His hands slipped down my body and parted my lips. The warm water enhanced the sensation of William's touch.

"You are so beautiful. You're the only woman I have ever loved," William whispered in my ear.

I moaned, turned around, and kissed my husband. My body shuddered as he cupped my breasts. His thumbs aroused my nipples as if unlocking the secrets to my soul. My knees almost buckled. I reached down and felt the hotness of his erection.

Out of the shower, he laid me down on the bed and lifted my legs. I was breathless as he knelt down and put his tongue between my thighs. My hips moved uncontrollably, pushing my clit against his tongue. Everything was moving faster now; his tongue connected to my body. My orgasm exploded, as volcanic pulsations radiated through me. I felt like my body would burst into flames at any moment. Then, no thoughts at all—I was in a world of bliss. I opened my eyes slowly, not wanting to leave this euphoria. I noticed a rosy tinge blossomed on the white skin of my freckled chest, a sure sign of my orgasm. "Stop," I panted. "I want you inside me."

He stood up, his erection still hard as a rock. He entered me, and I gasped with surprise and pleasure. He pressed against me, still standing, and his thrusts came faster. I looked down at his glistening cock moving in and out of my pussy and grew even more aroused. He pounded faster. "I'm going to come!" he cried.

He pumped repeatedly and then let out a moan and trembled. I felt the warmth of his orgasm radiate in my body. His thrusting slowed, and he collapsed on top of me. The weight of him felt good. We kissed gently for some time.

"I love you," he said, his eyes locked on mine as he stroked my hair.

"I love you," I replied as a rush of fondness and devotion filled my inner being.

I more than enjoyed making love with William. I knew he would like to have sex more often than we had been, but sometimes I was exhausted at the end of the evening, by a day filled with kids, chores, and life.

"I'm going to try to make more time for us to have sex," I promised him as I pulled him closer and squeezed his cock inside of me while kissing him harder.

Uncovering

We were alone, sitting in the outdoor hot tub. Ancient points of light dotted the black expanse above us, while the nearby ocean serenaded us with rhythmic waves breaking on the shore. William's sigh rose with the steam from the swirling waters. Since the trip back from the village to our hotel, with the exception of making love, William had been silent. His mind had been working, the wheels turning nuances, facts, thoughts, ideas, concepts, and questions over and over in his head. In our twenty-year marriage, I knew my husband pretty well and knew when to stay quiet and let him think things through. His sigh was usually a sign he had reached an impasse.

"You okay?" I asked.

"Yeah…we, uh, need to talk about what we saw or didn't see today."

"At the village, the Lacandón people?" I asked, to make sure we were on the same page, even though it was obvious.

"Yes. What did you notice?"

"Well, for starters, as I said then, it looked like we could have been in a village somewhere in Asia," I responded.

"Lehi; his wife, Sariah; his four sons, Laman, Lemuel, Nephi, Sam; and their sisters came from the Middle East, and the church teaches that the Native American peoples are direct descendants of Lehi and his family. They came from the Middle East, not over some land bridge from Asia. They are not supposed to look Asian."

"So maybe we have the location wrong," I offered.

"Actually, I think we have a bigger problem."

"The Book of Mormon or the whole church?" I queried.

"If the Book of Mormon is a fraud, well, then the whole church may be as well," William replied.

I knew what William was referring to; Joseph Smith, the first prophet of the church, had been given plates of gold by an angel. Engraved on these plates of gold were characters of a reformed Egyptian language, and they contained the writings of Lehi, his son Nephi, and the ancient prophets who followed them, all of whom lived on the American continent. I had heard it before. If the Book of Mormon was not what it claimed to be, then everything to do with the church could crumble.

"So what do we do?" I continued.

"When we get back home, I'll have to do more research to determine the origins of these people. Are they from the Middle East, as the church has emphatically stated, or are they from Asia, coming over an ancient land bridge?" William said, drifting as if out into space.

I looked up at the stars and thought for a moment about how ancient astronomers must have felt when they realized, contrary to long-held religious and scientific beliefs, that the Earth was not the center of the universe. Long-held beliefs and folklore versus science.

Home

Once we returned home, our family life quickly fell into place—work, kids, chores, and writing. One night, several weeks after our return, I was just finished getting ready for bed; William was already in bed, his laptop on his lap. I could tell by the look on his face that something was bothering him.

"Is everything okay?"

"Take a look at these," he said, pointing to an e-mail he had opened on his computer.

> Mr. Taylor,
>
> Concerning your question about American Indians being descendants of a lost tribe of Israel, there are no mitochondrial DNA or Y-chromosome data that support a biological connection between Middle Eastern and Native American populations, and the same is true of the classical blood-group marker and immune-gene data sets for the same populations. This fact alone should dispel any Mormon theories of the relatedness of Native Americans and ancient Jewish groups. In other words, the ideas put forward by you and other Mormon scholars simply don't stand up to examination, not if one looks at the empirical data.
> Sincerely,
> Dr. Lamarck

I turned to William. "You're kidding me."

"I wish I were. But wait; there's another e-mail you need to read."

William clicked on another e-mail from a Raffaella Peña, PhD, a scholar, professor, and senior research scientist in ancient languages from Yale University.

> Dear Mr. Taylor,
>
> Thank you for your interest in my research. As I mentioned to other leaders of your church and the research team at BYU, there is no scientific evidence that any spoken or written language of any Native American group originated from some form of a Hebraic language.

I let them know I was willing to share with them my research on the subject, "Origins of Native American Languages." My research has been published and reviewed, and I am more than willing to go over it with you. If you are interested, please contact my research assistant, Stephen Kaku. I cc'd him on this e-mail. If you have questions after reading my paper, please feel free to contact me again.

Best of luck on your quest,

R. Peña, PhD

PS: I just checked, and as far as I can tell, your BYU research team has not requested a copy of my research.

I sat there stunned. Neither of us said a word.

Finally, I broke the silence. "So now what?"

"I e-mailed both experts, asking for copies of their research and asked Dr. Peña if she would share with me who from BYU had contacted her."

"Good. What else can I do?" I asked.

"Make us reservations to fly to Utah."

William was respected and well connected in the church, so when I made a call to headquarters, asking for a meeting with leaders of the church, an audience was quickly granted.

Seeking Answers in Zion

We checked into our hotel in downtown Salt Lake City around noon. We had an appointment with a church leader—at this level, the leaders were called *general authorities*—and a few church researchers and one or two from BYU that afternoon.

I had only been to church headquarters once before. With all the money the church had, I would have thought their offices would be a little more updated. The white twenty-eight-story office building had been completed in 1972. The exterior still had a 1970s architectural look. The interior, although clean and neat, gave me the sense I had traveled back into the '70s. We sat there patiently waiting, lost in our thoughts while holding hands.

I turned to William. "Did we remember everything?"

He looked at me and let out a little laugh. "I hope so," he said, and he kissed me.

After a short wait, we were led into a conference room. We were introduced to two general authorities, Elder George Sorenson, who was one of the twelve apostles in the church, and four researchers, Brian Judkins and Kent Hayes from BYU and Gabriella Roh and Charleton Ogburn from FARMS. It was a little intimidating, but when I put my hand on William's, he gave it a reassuring squeeze back.

"I will offer a prayer," Elder George Sorenson, the apostle, said more than he asked.

As we all bowed our heads, I wondered if a prayer from an apostle would somehow be different.

We all said amen after what was a very short prayer.

For some reason, I was expecting something longer, primarily from an apostle—especially since rumor had it that these men had a direct hotline to God. Later, William told me it wasn't uncommon for general authorities to give very short and to-the-point prayers. Prayers were meant to give thanks and ask for assistance or guidance, not offer a sermon.

We went over our findings and showed them the e-mails we had received from Dr. Lamarck the geneticist and Dr. Peña. At the conclusion of our presentation, a few men set their pens down. Elder Sorenson took his glasses off, pulled a white handkerchief out of his suit-jacket pocket, and cleaned his glasses. The pause and silence seemed to go on for an eternity. He looked at his colleagues and then turned to us.

"Brother Taylor, you are highly thought of among the quorum of the twelve. Your name is on the short list for future leadership positions. Your skills in the courtroom, your knowledge of legal matters, your grasp of the gospel, and your public-speaking skills are well known."

He turned to me. "Sister Taylor, I wonder how good a lawyer you might have become. Fortunately, you decided to place family above all else. I understand from your college professors that they thought you had all the makings of a future judge, not to mention your success as a writer. We all know that a man is only as good as the woman who supports him. So thank you for all you do."

How much research and background information do they have on us? I wondered.

"So what do you think?" Elder Sorenson finally asked.

"About our discoveries, you mean?" William asked.

"Yes. I mean, where do we go from here?" Elder Sorenson asked.

"We were hoping we could find some answers," I said.

"Yes," William added. "We've tossed this matter over and over, trying to figure out an answer or an explanation for this puzzling research."

"I think with recent scientific advances in DNA research, the research from Dr. Lamarck is something the church has never had to grapple with," I interjected.

"There is some truth to your statement, Sister Taylor, and life was so much simpler even just a few years ago. You have both brought up good points. But let me ask you this   do you think there is a better church out there than our church?" Elder Sorenson asked.

William looked at me, and I could see something different in his eyes: hurt. I was unsure how to respond, and I think William felt the same way.

"Church leaders throughout the years have said if the first vision or the Book of Mormon are false, then the whole church collapses," I added softly, looking at William and not the other gentlemen in the room.

Elder Sorenson smiled at the two of us, then looked at his colleagues and then back at us. "We have considered what you have brought to our attention. We were aware of the research conducted by

Doctors Lamarck and Peña, whom you've communicated with, and we followed their research with great interest. We, the brethren, obviously are disappointed with their conclusions. We are doing our research here at BYU, and the investigation is still ongoing."

"Do you think you will come to a different conclusion?" I asked, curious to know because I wanted a logical explanation, something to restore my waning faith.

"The DNA study could take years, and as you know, BYU has one of the best language programs in the country. We have reviewed Dr. Peña's body of work. Even in her research paper, she did cite a few languages that changed rather quickly. Of course, we are considering her statement about Native American languages not being derived from a type of Hebrew."

"So the church has no scientific evidence to refute their peer-reviewed research?" William asked.

As William asked the question, I remembered Dr. Peña writing that no one from the church or BYU had asked for her study. Could she have been confused? Or did the church ask anonymously for a copy of her research?

"Not at this time," Elder Sorenson said.

"So is the church going to change its position on the statements from former general authorities?" I asked. *Revise history* is what I wanted to ask.

"As we all know, just because I say something, it doesn't mean it was inspired. We will look at everyone's statements and consider under what context they made them. Was it at General Conference, a meeting of some kind, or were they just giving their opinion? As we all know, sometimes folklore will take on a life of its own."

William and I looked at each other. He looked the way I felt: puzzled and sick to the stomach.

"I have to say I am disappointed," William said, and I nodded in agreement.

"I just ask that you have faith and be a little patient," Elder Sorenson said.

"Do you think that's what the Catholic Church said to Copernicus?" I asked.

"Galileo, you mean? And we are not going to jail you," Elder Sorenson said and smiled.

"That's reassuring," I said.

14

"As Rebecca already brought up, Joseph Smith stated that the Book of Mormon is the cornerstone of our religion and the most correct book," William pointed out. "The church stands or falls with the truthfulness of the Book of Mormon. I…I know I'm not telling you anything new," he added, his voice trailing off.

"That is true, and we are searching for answers, and many prayers are being offered for inspiration to bring an understanding to these important issues. I would ask both of you to look at the greater good and support the church brings to millions of lives. I would add that we have a number of researchers poring over the many passages where leaders of the church have talked about the Native Americans being descendants of the people of the Book of Mormon. It's possible that when they spoke, they were only giving their opinion and were not inspired by the Holy Ghost."

And just like that, the meeting was over. Elder Sorenson offered another short prayer.

As we stood, Elder Sorenson extended his hand and said, "I am sorry if you didn't get the answers you were seeking today. I hope you will not share your findings until further notice."

"Thanks," William said and then added gruffly, "We'll think about it."

With that, we were quickly whisked out of the room and into the elevator.

A Road Taken

We walked back to our hotel in silence, deep in thought. I could tell William was angry. He was right to feel frustrated and irritated; it was very disappointing not to reach a conclusion at our meeting with the church officials.

"How about we go for a workout, take our frustrations out on the machines, and then grab some dinner?" I suggested, breaking the silence and hoping to redirect William's building gall.

"That sounds good," he said through clenched teeth and feigning a smile.

I could sense something different in William's tone, something I'm not sure I had ever heard before. Maybe what I was sensing was a reflection of my feelings. His demeanor seemed much more than just disappointed, more like defeated, and William hated to lose.

After our workout, I thought about asking William if he wanted to join me in the shower to get his mind off the meeting and onto something more pleasurable, but I realized I was more hungry than horny. Not to mention we might never make it to dinner if we started down the lovemaking path.

Yes, I was disappointed, but I was not as committed to the church as William was; he had given his heart and soul to the church. After a workout and a shower, I felt better, and I think William did, too.

We were discussing the day's events in the restaurant while looking over the menu, when our young waitress, Annie, with long blond hair and a slight build, came over. "Sorry for the delay. What can our chef prepare for you tonight?" Annie asked with upbeat enthusiasm.

William smiled at me, a kind of Cheshire cat smile.

"I'll take the grilled salmon," I said.

"Excellent choice," our waitress responded.

"Would you recommend the salmon or filet mignon?" William asked.

"Boy, that's a tough one—not the filet mignon; I mean it's not tough. Ah, sorry, I'm babbling. Um…the salmon," Annie finally said.

"It must be good; I'll have the same," William said.

"You two are making this too easy," Annie said, smiling.

William flashed his *I've got a secret* smile at me again. "I love your enthusiasm," he said.

16

"Well, thank you. My mother always said the only thing we have control over is our attitude. So why not choose to be happy?"

"Excellent advice," I said.

"What type of wine would you recommend?" William asked.

It was as if a bolt of lightning just landed near our table out of a clear-blue sky. I never saw this question coming. I sat up, startled. William's question about a wine recommendation seemed to be one of those totally surreal, almost dreamlike, moments. I have to admit that not much left me speechless, but this moment did. Partly because we were devout Mormons and did not drink alcohol, and partly because, quite frankly, I wasn't sure if I had heard William correctly…or if I had been transported into some movie scene. Although it wasn't unusual for us to go to dinner with non-Mormon friends or colleagues of William who would order drinks, we never participated.

"I'll have to ask my manager. I recently started here, and I don't drink. I'll be right back," Annie said apologetically.

She was about to leave, when William said, "Annie, I trust your manager has good taste, and we trust his judgment. So just bring us whatever he recommends."

"Sure, okay." She smiled and was gone.

"William, wine? Really?"

"Why not?"

"Have you ever had wine before?" I asked.

"Nope. This will be the first time."

I was silent, unsure what to say and unsure whether I was going to have a glass of wine with him.

"It's a crock," William added softly.

I looked at this man I loved more than anything in the world. He was throwing in the towel. "The church?" I asked knowingly.

"Yes."

Tears stung at my eyes. I trusted William with all my heart and soul. I would follow him anywhere. He had reached a decision, and I wanted to break down and cry. I knew what he was saying was true. I was gripped with fear of the unknown.

"The wine is to celebrate," William said, breaking the silence.

"Do you think we can get our tithing back?" I asked in jest.

This brought him a big grin and a laugh and made me feel reassured.

"Now that is an interesting question and would be interesting

17

litigation. A church knowingly misleading its members," William said thoughtfully.

"You're going a little rogue, don't you think?"

I knew William, and once he had come to a conclusion based on facts, not on hope and faith, he moved on pretty quickly. My mind felt like a whirlwind of emotions.

"I guess you could look at it that way."

There was another moment of silence as I gazed around the room, a little self-conscious.

"But I kind of like it," I said at last, winking.

"I love you," he said, catching me off guard. My eyes burned, and tears welled up.

"I love you, too, William, and I suppose I was kind of expecting today's outcome—even though I hoped they would have answers. I may have lost the church, but I still have my husband and family."

"I agree. I've given it much thought, and I'm afraid the church isn't quite what it says it is."

"The veil removed?" I asked.

"Yes, the wizard exposed," he answered with conviction.

"I guess I'm also ready to try new things," I added.

"Guilt-free?"

Before I could answer, Annie approached us. "My manager recommended this, a 2006 Storming the Castle, Russian River Valley Pinot Noir," she said as she held out the bottle.

"Perfect," William said proudly, setting down his glass.

She opened our bottle with a little difficulty—not like we could have done any better—and poured William a sample in his glass. He swirled the red wine in his glass like we had seen our friends do and took a sip. I was watching this all with fascination, especially to see if William would give away any clues that this was his first taste of alcohol.

"This is excellent," he said.

Just then, a tall man appeared at our table.

"Hello, I'm John, the manager. I meant to come over earlier."

"That's quite all right, John, the manager," I said.

William grinned at me.

"I wanted to explain. A gentleman by the name of John Youngsmith makes this wine. He works as a lawyer by day and a winemaker by night. This wine is a classic Russian River Pinot Noir. It has a hint of ripe cherry right down to its silky, inviting texture."

"It is an excellent wine, and thank you for the recommendation," William said.

With that, both our waitress and John excused themselves. I picked up my glass and looked at it for a moment. "Cheers," I said as I raised it toward William's.

"To new beginnings," he said.

We clinked our glasses. I looked at William to see if he had any sense of guilt. Our faith in our religion was unraveling in slow motion right before our eyes. *Is getting a bottle of wine really what we should be doing?* I thought as guilt accompanied by a sense of loss wove its way into my being.

"How did it taste?" I asked before I took my sip.

"I suppose the way Pinot Noir is supposed to taste. See for yourself," William said, raising his glass to his lips.

I did the same. I inhaled, assessing the aroma of the wine. There was definitely a hint of cherry. I took a small sip. It warmed my throat all the way down and then into my bloodstream. I felt relaxed almost immediately.

"Wow," I said.

Caution to the Wind

After dinner and our bottle of wine, we found ourselves getting a little passionate in the elevator of our hotel. I was wearing a relatively short skirt because I knew William couldn't keep his hands off my legs. All those hours in the gym paid off, keeping my husband a happy man.

The elevator came to a stop. *Our floor already*, I thought as the door opened.

"Oh" was all I could get out as an elderly couple stepped in.

"We're sorry to interrupt," the man said, smiling.

His wife seemed a little embarrassed. "Honey, maybe we should catch the next one."

"Oh no, that's not necessary. Come on in," William said, taking my hand.

"We can wait," I said, maybe just a little tipsy.

William looked at me and gave me a wry look.

We were laughing hysterically once we finally got our keycard to work and tumbled into our room.

"Seriously, I can't believe you said we could wait," William said, laughing.

"Oh, hush. Find us a movie to watch while I change into something more comfortable," I responded as I walked to the bathroom.

"Any special requests?" William asked as I was closing the door.

"Your choice, baby," I replied and shut the door.

I freshened up a little bit and changed into my thigh-high black nylons, sexy G-string, and a see-through negligee. It was common during our time away from the kids for me to pack a sexy outfit, and usually we would rent an adult movie, something to spice up our sex lives.

When I came out of the bathroom, William was under the covers with the remote control in his hand.

He looked at me and said, "You sexy goddess, get over here," patting the side of the bed next to him.

"What did you find for us to watch?"

"Something a little different."

"Oh, good."

"I think you'll like it," William said, pointing the remote at the television. "God, you look sexy."

William started the movie as I got into bed. "What's it about?" I asked.

"Amateur movies about wives living out their fantasies."

"Amateur?"

"Yeah, supposedly you can contact this website and tell them your fantasy, and they will set it up. If everyone agrees, they will film it for this kind of video."

"Really?"

William pointed the remote at the television and pressed a button. "I think so," he said as the movie started on the flat-screen.

The first scene unfolded with a not-very-good-looking older man and a beautiful, voluptuous younger wife. Either he was wealthy, or these were actors pretending to be amateurs. Her fantasy was to have sex with a porn star. The guy she was going to have sex with was not my type and not very good looking, but he was well endowed.

"Does she turn you on?" I asked.

"No, she seems too fake for my taste. What about the guy for you?"

"No, not at all," I answered.

We watched as the couple on the screen got straight to business.

"Do you think they're a couple?" I asked as my hand was making its way down past his abdomen.

"Seems hard to believe. I just wish the director or host or producer or announcer whoever he is would shut up," William said.

"I know; I don't care to hear his commentary, either."

The first scene ended, and the next one started. This scene featured a gorgeous, voluptuous brunette and her dorky, ugly husband

"No way they are together in real life," William chimed in.

We were kissing now, stopping every so often to watch more of the film.

"Not much of a story either. Just straight to the action," I added.

This woman's fantasy was to have sex with two porn stars.

"Double her pleasure," William commented.

"Seems like a lot of work."

William laughed. I kept my hand on his rock-hard erection, and I was getting pretty wet myself.

When they finally finished, the poor woman looked really spent.

"See, I told you that would be a lot of work," I muttered.

The next scene showed a middle-aged couple. The woman looked as though she was in her late thirties, maybe early forties. Her husband seemed a little older.

"She looks nervous to me," I said.

"She does, doesn't she?"

"What do you think her fantasy is?"

"Three guys?" William asked more than answered and kissed me.

It wasn't three guys; the older brunette told the host that her fantasy was to have sex with a well-endowed black man. A few minutes later, a black man came into the shot. They talked for a few minutes, and her nervousness seemed to increase. Her voice sounded a little shaky.

"She seems really nervous now," William interjected.

"This couple does seem real," I added while stroking William's hard cock.

The black guy sat next to the woman. He started caressing her leg, and then they kissed.

The woman on the screen looked over at her husband. "Are you sure?" she asked.

He must have nodded offscreen because she went back to kissing her fantasy in the flesh.

His hand was now pulling aside her G-string. She was moaning as her hand unbuttoned his shirt and rubbed his chest and down his washboard abs.

While all this was happening on the video, William's hand was repeating what he saw on the screen. I was as wet as William was hard.

On-screen, the man's hand moved to her blouse, and he slowly unbuttoned each button, kissing her more passionately with each button he undid.

They were standing now, and she had moved her hands down to his belt and was unlatching the buckle. He removed her blouse and kissed her again. He took off his shirt, showing his chiseled chest and then went to work on freeing her breasts from her black lace bra.

Once free of their restraints, her large breasts, now without any support, let gravity take over. They were definitely all natural.

"She reminds me of you," William said while gently rubbing between my thighs.

I thought for a moment he must be reading my mind, because I was turned on thinking the same thing.

22

"Oh, thanks. Her saggy breasts reminded you of me?" I said. We both laughed.

"No, not at all. Besides kind of looking like you, something about her innocence, reluctance; all I know is it's turning me on," he continued.

I looked at the woman on-screen, her white, milky skin like mine, as she reached into his boxers and pulled it out. It was so big in her hand. He had his fingers inside her. She was moaning louder.

Then, from deep within me, my orgasm welled up; my body tensed and then exploded like a volcano erupting, releasing some long-stored pressure. Warm waves of pleasure radiated through my body. I didn't even have time to push William's fingers away. I wanted him inside me. My hand stroked the length of his cock. I could sense he was about to come also.

"Wait. Not yet. I want to taste you," William said, pushing my hand away.

"No, I'm too sensitive."

We kissed for a little longer. William would push my hand away anytime it was on his erection for too long. My body ached for him. I wanted him inside me.

He worked his way down my body after kissing me for several minutes. I was warm and tingly all over. I could feel another orgasm building as William worked his magic with his tongue.

I opened my eyes briefly to look at the television. The brunette was on her knees, and she had her interracial lover's big cock in her mouth. His hands were on the back of her head.

What would it be like? Another man's cock in my mouth and my husband watching?

It looked like he was going to come. He was moaning so much. She looked up at him with an inviting look; she wanted to please him.

Without any further warning, I was coming again. A thought of *I want to be his* flashed into my mind without warning as I was lifting my hips and grinding into William's face. He thrust his tongue inside me. I finally had to push William's head and tongue away; my body was so sensitive. Shockwaves were pulsating through my body. It seemed like it was one never-ending orgasm. I was exhausted. A sense of shame started to creep in, but I shut it down before it could take hold.

No guilt, remember, I told myself. *I can't believe I wanted to be the woman in the video. I wanted to be used.*

23

My head rested on William's chest as I tried to catch my breath. My body was still trembling with aftershocks. This had been one of the most intense orgasms I'd ever had. My attention turned to the interracial couple on the screen who were changing positions.

My hand stroked William's erection again. He seemed bigger than normal, and I could tell he was getting close to having his orgasm.

"Do you think you could ever have sex with a black guy?" he asked, breaking the silence.

The question caught me off guard. Had he somehow read my mind? Did I blurt something out in the throes of my orgasm? Now guilt tried to take the place of shame. I reassured myself I had not said anything. The question also surprised me in part. Despite my fantasy of being used by the man on the screen, I had never really considered ever having sex with someone other than my husband. Growing up as a member of the Mormon church, interracial relationships were taboo. I know it sounds crazy nowadays, but that is what the church was like when I was a little girl. It was taboo—very, very wrong. William and I were both of European descent, and everyone I had dated had been a so-called Mormon wholesome white. I know, hearing that out loud sounds so wrong now. So my answer surprised me.

"I would pretend he had a great tan," I answered.

I kissed William's chest and then started kissing lower and lower.

"No," William said, pulling me back by my shoulders.

"Why? But I want to."

"No. I won't last."

"That's okay; I want it."

"No, I want to be inside of you."

William had told me once that since he knew that I really didn't like the taste of cum, and the thought of me gagging made coming in my mouth a turnoff, he liked blow jobs only to a point. On one occasion when I was at the pharmacy, waiting for a prescription to be filled, I was browsing the aisles, and I noticed a colorful box of flavored condoms—strawberry, cola, banana, vanilla, grape, and my personal favorite, chocolate. I was so excited with my find, we tried them that night and had fun with them. On the nights I was in the mood to please William orally, I would have a flavored condom ready. Unfortunately, we didn't have the condoms with us on this trip.

We kissed, and William rolled me onto my back and spread my legs. When he slowly entered me, I shuddered with small gasps of

24

pleasure.

"I love you," I whispered.

"You are my true love."

We stayed there kissing and moaning. William was moving his hips; my legs were spread, and my hips were trying to cling to his body. I wanted all of William in me.

"Oh my God," William said. "I am so turned on imagining that is you."

I stole a glimpse at the TV. The interracial couple was in the missionary position. Her legs were spread open. His dark hips were moving up and down in long motions between her thighs. I was so turned on watching her raise her hips to meet his thrusts. Her paleness contrasting his dark-brown skin. Her body melting into his. It seemed to me like she wanted all of him inside of her. She was coming, pushing her white hips up, grinding against him.

I started to come, too.

"Oh baby, I'm going to come!" William called out.

I wrapped my legs around him, grinding against his pelvic bone and heightening my stimulation. We came together. Intense pleasure radiated into all parts of my body. Lost in the moment of having no thoughts at all, I lay there spent, as soft tremors floated through my body. I wanted more. More pleasure, another orgasm; but rest won out, and soon we were falling asleep in a lovers' embrace.

A Letter

Nearly a year had passed since our adventure in Salt Lake City, and our nonchurch life had returned to normal. There had been no word from the church or BYU. We had numerous discussions, wondering what our next step should be with the information we had. Finally we decided we could no longer live a lie and felt it was best that we officially leave the church. So we sent a letter requesting that our names be removed from the church membership records.

Not long after, we received a letter from the church headquarters in Salt Lake City, addressed to Brother William and Sister Rebecca Taylor. I held the letter in my hand and wondered if this was the confirmation that our request to have our names removed from the records of the church had been honored.

I thought about opening the letter. Then I thought I should call William and see if he wanted me to open the letter or wait for him to get home so we could open it together.

I decided to wait for William. I wasn't sure if this was a cause to celebrate, yet a longing and a sadness swept through me. I thought about where our journey had taken us. To give up on your beliefs and, more importantly, to decide that your entire religion was based on untruths was an even more earth-shattering decision.

William got home, we had dinner, and I finally put the kids to bed.

"I thought about calling or texting you earlier today to let you know a letter from church headquarters arrived today," I said, trying to hide my angst.

William, who was sitting at his desk in the study, said, "Oh wow," putting his reading glasses down.

I walked over to him, picked up the legal files he was reading, and set them on the desk.

"Trotsky would be more appropriate reading," I said. I took the envelope from behind my back and held it up. "From the First Presidency."

"So this is it?" he said.

"Really? That's all? Just a 'so this is it'?"

"I know. I'm not sure how I feel. It seems kind of final," he said.

"Well, what's done is done. This was mailed three days ago," I said, double-checking the dated postage.

"What if I'm wrong about the church?"

"What if *we're* wrong, you mean? Remember, we both came to the same conclusion."

He smiled grimly. "Well, open it."

I reached for the letter opener I had slid into my back pocket.

"Holy mackerel, you mean to tell me you had a dagger with you all this time?"

I opened the letter and drawled, "You're lucky you behaved, comrade." I said this in my best Russian accent.

I moved to the side of his chair so William and I could read the letter together.

> Dear Brother and Sister Taylor,
>
> We are in receipt of your letter, requesting that your membership be removed from the records of the church.
>
> I would like to request a meeting with you both. I will be in the Los Angeles area next weekend, October 16. I have limited availability that day. We could meet at the Los Angeles Mission headquarters next to the Los Angeles Temple.
>
> Please give my secretary, Brother Spencer, a call at the number below.
>
> Sincerely,
>
> Elder Joseph Bidamon Smith

"That's somewhat anticlimactic," William said disappointedly.

"Why do you think they want to talk with us?"

"The suspense builds. It could be for a number of reasons."

"Do you have any second thoughts?" I asked, searching William's face for any sign of doubt.

"I wish I did, but there is nothing to support the church. In fact, the evidence we've uncovered is to the contrary," he said, his voice trailing off.

Behind Closed Doors

Life and kids seemed to have a habit of getting in the way of uninhibited, spontaneous, unrestrained sex. With the demands of kids, chores, work, and family, sexual intimacy took a back seat. It had been a while since our adventure in Cancun and my promise to make more time for lovemaking.

One morning I woke up in the middle of an erotic dream. I was bent over William's desk, my church dress pulled up over my head and my black pumps still on. I was breathless and getting dizzy. I reached down to feel his hardness.

"I want it," I moaned.

He slid his hand between my legs. I moaned and backed up into his hand.

"No," he said. As he pushed my hips against the desk, he placed a firm hand on the small of my back. He was being aggressive, and I liked it.

I moaned again and begged, "Please."

He grabbed a handful of my hair, softly at first and then pulled it tight. He kissed my neck and then plunged into me. I gasped with surprise and pleasure. I was lost in the rhythm as he rocked me, pumping faster and faster. He was about to come, and so was I.

"Oh my God, I'm going to—" I cried out.

The warm sensations of my orgasm filled my body. As I looked to the side, William was sitting in a chair, watching. Panic replaced my sense of satisfaction. Whoever was behind me and had taken hold of my hair and entered me was not William. His moaning voice was familiar. The comprehension that I was not having sex with my husband startled me out of my dream.

Throughout the day, I had flashes of the look on William's face in my dream—the panic, the naughtiness of it all, the shame, the arousal I felt, yet I wanted William badly. I had resisted the temptation during the day to satisfy myself to the emotions and images of my dream. Instead, I held off my self-gratification, waiting instead for the real thing with William.

The kids were finally in bed. William had offered to read to them that night, and when at last he came to bed, he found me dressed in a sexy red teddy.

28

I know it's kind of a contradiction, but I love sex with my husband. I love to feel sexy in lingerie, and I know how much it turns William on. I just run out of enthusiasm at the end of the day. During the day I find myself on the Victoria's Secret website, shopping for outfits.

"Wow! Is it Father's Day? Wait, oh shoot—Valentine's Day?" he quipped.

It was a running joke because three of our kids, Connor, Luke, and Miranda, had March birthdays, and if you do the math, nine months from March is around Father's Day. Jessica and Hannah had November birthdays; you guessed it, Valentine's Day. So my friends would tease me that William and I only had sex on either Father's Day or Valentine's Day. I suppose the red teddy may have confused matters for William.

"We can pretend," I said, patting his pillow.

William tore off his clothes in a single motion.

"Maybe we should get a phone booth for the bedroom." I giggled at images of Superman from my childhood jumping into a phone booth, changing from the mild-mannered Clark Kent to Superman.

He was getting quite adept at the shedding of clothes at a moment's notice. Soon our naked bodies were intertwined. William kissed me passionately. Our hands roamed all over each other's bodies. Our tongues met and danced, the sensation heightening.

I pushed him over onto his back.

"I want you in my mouth," I said.

William could only manage to let out a groan of surrender.

I kissed and licked William's neck, while he rubbed my body as low as his arms could reach. Then I moved to his nipples, my tongue flicking lightly back and forth. He was moving his hips, and I could feel his erection against my leg. I was so aroused by my dream, I was afraid the pressure from William's rock-hard thigh rubbing against my clit would make me come.

"Did you lock the door?" I asked, interrupting our foreplay.

"Nope, but I will," he said, jumping out of bed, his erection leading the way, swaying back and forth like a dowsing rod searching, in this case for a fertile field to plant his seed.

God, he has a beautiful body, I thought. William worked out at a gym six days a week, and it paid off.

"Mission accomplished," he said with a satisfied smile. "Does my fair maiden require anything else from her humble servant?" he continued in his best British accent.

"Yes, come hither, and let your queen satisfy her king," I responded in character.

William lay down on the bed. We kissed, and my hands rubbed the muscles on his back and shoulders. I pushed him onto his back and worked my way down and teased him, letting my long hair brush against his erection while placing kisses all around his throbbing manhood. Finally, I took him in my hand and gave his erection a kiss. Looking up at William with my sultry eyes, I licked and teased with my tongue and mouth.

William's hands were at his sides, gripping the sheets. He was groaning and moving his hips with motions of encouragement. I held my breath and listened to make sure none of the kids was awake. I finally took his erection into my mouth.

"Mmm, somebody is excited. I can taste your precum," I said before returning to my job at hand or mouth or both. I bobbed up and down. William grew harder and bigger. I could tell he was getting close.

"Stop!" he said, pushing my head away. "You're going to make me come."

"That's the point," I said, giving his erection a squeeze.

"No, come up here," he pleaded.

"Aww, no fun."

So I acquiesced. Besides the fantasy of pleasuring William to the point of his total satisfaction, his coming in my mouth was not nearly the same as the reality of what transpired in real life, with all the smells and tastes. So I sauntered back up, kissing William's body along the way. We lay there entwined, kissing and hands exploring. After a little while, he rolled me over on my back. He kept kissing me, and I spread my legs. I was ready for him; I wanted to feel him deep inside of me. Instead of entering me, he worked his way down with his lips and tongue—if I had to admit, a bit quicker than I'd done with him.

It wasn't long before he found my magical, engorged button of nerves. I was moaning and moving my hips, grinding my clitoris against his tongue. I was getting close. I took control of his head so I could adjust the pressure, and it wasn't long before my body tensed, and my orgasm rippled through my body. A warm rush of endorphins soothed my body and soul. His tongue flicking my sensitive clit, I pushed his head away.

"Okay, that's enough," I said between breaths.

30

We kissed. I could taste myself on William's lips and tongue. I reached down, his throbbing erection begging for satisfaction. I spread my legs and guided him inside me. The pleasure sensations in my body went wild at the thought and feeling of William inside of my most private and restricted area only for my husband.

"Oh God, baby, you feel so good," he said.

I was grinding my pelvis against his as he slowly moved around inside me. I wanted him deep inside me and spread my legs further apart.

"Do you ever think about that night?" he asked.

"What night?"

"The night in Salt Lake City," William whispered.

"What about it?" I asked, unsure of where he was going.

He was slowly moving in and out of me now. "The video. The black guy was having sex with the woman, your twin, while her husband watched," he said softly.

"Oh, that."

"Yeah, that one," he said, a little distant.

Had I hurt his feelings? I hadn't thought about it. Without warning, the contrasting images of his dark skin against her white body flashed before my eyes. Her hips were moving to take him deeper. The carnal sensation I wanted to take him deeper. The way she spread her legs, the same way I was spreading my legs now. I was totally aroused again. I could feel another orgasm building. I worried William might be upset if he knew it turned me on to imagine the black man was inside of me. His big, black cock inside of me only made me wetter. God, it turned me on.

"Do you?" I asked, putting the ball back in his court.

William was thrusting hard now. "Yes, and I imagine that is you in the video."

"Does that turn you on?" I asked, getting more aroused and wetter, if that was even possible.

"Oh God, yes, it does," he moaned.

William was pumping faster and harder now. "I'm going to come," he said, his voice muted as his face buried in my neck.

"Me too, baby," I moaned and thrust my hips, taking all of William inside of me.

His body tensed, and he groaned. Then, knowing he was coming inside of me, I had my second orgasm of the night.

Just a Fantasy?

As I was lying there in my husband's arms, slowly coming out of my euphoric haze, I started to hope the kids hadn't heard us and then think about what I needed to do the next day. The thought jumped from nervous butterflies in my stomach to my mind without warning.

"It's just a fantasy, right?" I nervously asked as the thought turned to words.

"What's that?" William asked.

"What you said," I replied.

"When?" William asked, running his hands through my hair.

"When we were making love. You talked about the interracial couple in the cuckold video and that being me."

"Oh, that. Yes, of course. Why?" he said, trying to reassure me.

"Because you know I am a one-man woman," I told him, giving him a kiss.

"I know that," he said, trying to reassure me. "It's just a fantasy."

"I need only you," I said, my head on his chest as my hand unconsciously played with his nipple.

He laughed a little while I stroked his chest. "It did turn me on to think that was you in that video," he admitted.

"Really? What about it turned you on so much?" I was still concerned that he might be upset by how turned on I was, not to mention how he might react to the guilt and shame I felt at the thought of some stranger using my body and giving him the pleasure I reserved for my husband. I realized I was rattled by the thought that some other man had turned me sexually.

"Did it turn you on?" he asked, now turning the question on me.

I wasn't exactly sure how to respond. "Yeah, I guess it did turn me on. Maybe mostly by the idea it turned you on."

"I could tell," he said softly.

"You could?"

"Not to be too graphic, but you were wet, really wet, and I don't remember you coming so...what's the word? Passionately."

"Really?" I had wondered if my body had given me away so obviously.

"Yes, really. So what turned you on about it?"

"I don't know. The taboo of it, I guess," I offered thoughtfully.

"For me, it was because the woman looked so much like you. Combined with you getting turned on, the whole thing was just a really big turn-on. It sort of triggered something in me. I think mostly because I hadn't ever seen you react in that way. So turned on, so sexual."

"And you keep thinking about it," I stated as much as asked.

"Yep, it still turns me on to think about," he said, almost in a whisper.

I was searching his eyes for something, some clue. "You'd want to watch me with another man?" I asked, a little afraid his answer might be a resounding *Yes! Yes, we should do this*. Yet my body, with a mind of its own, was getting turned on again. From some dark, secret well of conscientiousness, there was a twinge of desire.

"I told you the thought or fantasy of it turns me on and especially how your body gives away your secret desires," he said.

"Are you gay?" I blurted out. I wanted to take it back. I was sure he was going to get angry.

"No, baby," he said with a laugh, "I'm not gay."

"Okay, sorry; it just came out." But I still wondered why a man would have a fantasy of another man making love to his wife. I thought men were uncomfortable around other naked men.

"That's okay. I suppose that's a natural question," he said.

We lay in silence for a little while. The images of the video danced through my mind, causing a vortex of emotions I didn't intellectually understand, even though my body seemed to interpret them for me.

William broke the silence. "I think it is, in part, that we are venturing on a new voyage, an exploration of truth. I just wonder if, when sharing the love of my life—in this case, my wife—sexually, as in the video, there also comes a sense of freedom."

"Freedom? What about jealousy?"

"That's sort of what I mean. I think for you to be spontaneously turned on by someone new is natural, and it doesn't make me jealous. Sort of like I'm not jealous when you do things with your friends," William said.

"Doing things with my friends like a girls' night out is completely different than having sex with someone."

"What about your last book tour, when your publisher and agent were there for the weekend in San Francisco?"

"Seriously, with Adrienne?" I asked.

33

"Yes, I didn't feel any sense of jealousy then."

"Adrienne is a woman," I reminded him.

"I know and a lesbian."

"Oh my God!" I said, laughing.

"And a gorgeous lesbian at that. Still no jealousy," William said, hoping to make his point.

"You're crazy."

We both laughed.

"I might feel objectified," I thought out loud.

"Really?"

"Maybe…wouldn't it be sort of like live porn?"

"I guess amateur porn versus professional porn, but still it's only a fantasy," William added.

"Are all black men that big?"

"Hmm…curiosity, I see."

"Well—" I responded weakly.

"Having been an athlete all my life and taking showers after practice and games, I would say not always, but—" He hesitated.

"But what?" I asked, now curious.

"Generally, I would say yes but not hung-like-a-horse bigger."

Neither of us said anything. I assumed that William was as lost in thought as I was. The image of the woman in the video replayed in my mind. I was getting horny again, and as my hand moved down from his torso to his groin, I could tell he was, too.

A Heated Debate

William and I were sitting in the lobby of the stake president's office, waiting for our scheduled appointment with the apostle, Elder Smith. William was dressed in a navy-blue suit with a white shirt and a matching tie from Saks, and I was in a conservative, flowered blue-and-white dress and black flats. William was looking at his phone, scrolling through work e-mails, and I was reading through my latest historical novel manuscript about the Pueblo Indian Revolt of 1680.

The door opened, and a tall, thin man in his midthirties dressed in a black suit, white shirt, and a black-and-white striped tie walked over to William and extended his hand.

"Brother Taylor," he said, extending his hand first to William before he offered his hand to me. "Sister Taylor. I'm Brother Brown. Thank you for your patience. I apologize for the wait. Please follow me."

He pointed us in the direction of the open door. William led the way, and I followed. In the room behind a desk sat Elder Smith.

Elder Smith rose and nodded. "Brother Taylor, Sister Taylor. Thank you so much for meeting with me tonight. I apologize for the wait."

"Not a problem," William said.

"Brother Brown, thank you; that will be all."

Brother Brown gently shut the door behind him.

"Please have a seat," Elder Smith said, gesturing toward the seats in front of the desk.

There was a moment of uncomfortable silence, because both William and I were a little unsure of what to say or do in front of an apostle of the church. Elder Smith was next in line to be president and prophet of the church. He was also a direct descendant of Hyrum Smith, brother of the first prophet and founder of the church, Joseph Smith, Jr.

"I appreciate that both of you took time out of your busy schedules to spend some time with me tonight," he said, breaking the silence.

"We're happy to meet with you, Elder Smith," William said. It was only partially true.

"If it is all right with the two of you, I'd like to offer a prayer to invite the Spirit to our meeting tonight."

"Sure," William responded. I just nodded and bowed my head.

I had always been curious—when an apostle of the church offered a prayer, would there be some kind of mystical energy you could feel? As Elder Smith closed his prayer, he seemed tired, and I didn't feel anything different.

"Brother and Sister Taylor, the prophet Gordon B. Hinckley asked that I meet with you regarding your letter requesting to have your names and ordinances removed from the records of the church."

"We didn't mean to put anyone through any extra hoops," William answered.

"Well, usually, this type of thing is a formality, but your circumstances are slightly different."

"Oh? How so?"

"The brethren are all aware of your research, and we have some concerns."

"I didn't realize that," I interjected.

"I am curious that if an ordinary couple like us can go down to Central America, observe what we saw, note the inconsistencies, and then ask questions of the science community culminating in our discouraging conclusion, why hasn't the church?" William said.

"You understand that we wanted to prove the Book of Mormon to be true, not the other way around, right?" I added.

"First, you underestimate yourselves. You are far too modest and anything but 'an ordinary couple.' Now with that being said, most of what goes through to the church research department is usually anti-Mormon recycled nonsense. Occasionally we get a letter from an overenthusiastic member stating something to the effect that they have discovered the Book of Mormon lands. The majority of the time there is no scholastic, historical, scientific, or even spiritual support for these claims. On the off chance we get a request for clarification such as yours that has merit, then these requests are usually raised as high in church leadership and scholarship as they need to go before being resolved. A research team had been following the DNA research of Dr. Lamarck, and we were disappointed with his findings. At a snail's pace and with all the optimism of the tortoise in the children's tale about the tortoise and the hare, we march forward," Elder Smith confessed.

"So did you ask us here because you have some clarification?" William asked.

More than a little surprised by his tone and straightforwardness, I

36

gave William a look. He ignored me and held Elder Smith's gaze.

"For some questions and/or requests for clarification, there are no answers. At least not at the moment," Elder Smith said.

William shot back, "The church maintains the position that we are not just one of many churches, but that we are the one and only true church on the face of the planet, solar system, and the universe, and maybe more."

"That is true," Elder Smith interjected.

"Yet the foundation of this truth is based on the Book of Mormon—and it may not be true."

"That's not what I am saying," Elder Smith responded, clearly getting irritated.

"The scientific evidence contradicts with what the church teaches, and that is that the Book of Mormon is an actual and accurate historical record and that the Native American Indians—North, Central, and South—are direct descendants of the people of the Book of Mormon. Frankly, what the church teaches does not hold water. More simply put, it is not true," William said, taking a breath.

"Now, Brother and Sister Taylor, as graduates of BYU Law School, you both know that the absence of evidence does not necessarily prove that the church doctrines are untrue. We are looking at the possibility of a limited geographical region, and we are confident that science will eventually support the authenticity of the Book of Mormon."

"An appeal to ignorance and shifting the evidence as some shell game? Really, Elder Smith? Is this the best argument the church has to offer?"

The debate went on like this for more than an hour. I know William, and he is the only person I would want defending my life in a debate. It's not like he set out to prove the church wrong. Instead, he sought to find a way to protect the church by proving it was all true. He was trying to find an answer where there was none. When he had exhausted all possibilities, William turned to the Foundation for Ancient Research and Mormon Studies in search of help, guidance, and, hopefully, answers.

Finally, Elder Smith pounded his fist on the desk, startling us both. William eased back into his seat.

"Okay, Brother Taylor, let's just assume you are correct. What else is better out there? What church is better than ours?" Elder Smith asked, clearly tired and agitated.

I looked at William. He was staring at Elder Smith, and their eyes were locked in a death stare. Finally, Elder Smith looked down in defeat.

"That's it? What else is better?" William demanded.

There was a long pause. It seemed like all the oxygen had been suctioned from the room. No one seemed to be breathing, and there was a dead stillness to everything.

"Elder Smith, please honor our request to remove our names from the records of the church membership. Come on, baby, let's go."

I looked at Elder Smith, and somehow he looked older now, frail and dejected.

I held out my hand. "Elder Smith, thank you."

He looked up and smiled. "Thank you, Sister Taylor." Then he turned to William. "I'm sorry, Brother Taylor."

William extended his hand and shook Brother Smith's hand. "Have a safe trip back, Elder Smith. I mean that sincerely, and I am sorry, too."

And just like that, it was over. A few weeks later, we received in the mail a letter from the First Presidency stating that "regretfully" and per our request, our names had been removed as members of the church. The finality of the message in the letter hit both of us like a powerful wave. What now? Our church friends, some quickly and others more slowly, distanced themselves. William and I started arguing a little more, and as I look back, I think we were drifting. Not necessarily apart, but a centerpiece of our lives was removed, and we had yet to replace it.

Exploration

The sun rose the next morning, and then the next, and then the next. Life moved on. William and I set out on an exploration of other religions and practices. Our sex life was full as we began to branch out into different forms of role-playing. William often brought up how turned on he would get at the thought of watching me with another man.

Finally, one day as we were lying in bed, I asked him the question that had been on my mind for weeks. "Is that all you fantasize about? Me with another man?"

"No," he answered quietly.

"Do you want to sleep with another woman? Is that why you bring this up so often?"

"No—why? Where did that come from?" William said as he turned and looked at me.

"Well, you keep talking about how you would like to watch me with another man."

"Yeah, I do, because it turns me on," he said a little defensively.

"But why? Is that the only way you can get off?" I asked, annoyed and concerned.

"I'm not sure, but it just does."

"If you want me to have the experience with other men, wouldn't it work the other way too—you with another woman?"

"No, I get satisfaction from the fantasy of watching you get pleased by a hot, hung guy," he said, more defensively than thoughtfully.

"Now it's a 'hot, hung' guy? How often do you have these fantasies?"

"I'm not sure how that makes any sense or what that has to do with this fantasy," he said.

"I'm not sure much makes sense anymore." I was a little angry, bitter, and hurt. I felt like I wasn't enough.

"I suppose this gets back to our commitment to ignore everything we've learned about philosophy, love, romance, capitalism, reality, and perception, as well as our search or commitment to exploring it for ourselves," William said.

We lay there in silence, motionless. I was resentful and confused. Questions swirled in my mind. *Wasn't I good enough for William? Did he want someone else? Why was he stuck on wanting to watch me have sex with another man?* Even though I thought about it from time to time, the interracial video wasn't *all* I thought about. I didn't realize it at the time, but I began to avoid sex with my husband.

Prying Eyes

There were times when I wandered into William's office and felt I had caught him looking at something on the Internet or doing something on his computer he didn't want me to see, because he quickly clicked away from whatever it was he was doing.

William usually took his laptop with him everywhere, but on this occasion, he was going on a quick one-day trip to San Francisco to meet with a new client. He had also recently purchased a new tablet and felt he could get by without his laptop. It was on this occasion my curiosity got the best of me. I opened up William's laptop and entered his password. I immediately opened his browser to look at the browsing history on his computer, and I was surprised. Surprised, but not surprised, I guess; I saw what I expected to see—video of women having sex with a black man. Then I noticed something about the women. They all in some way could have been me. Then another thought occurred to me. *Had William knowingly let me catch him, hoping I would do exactly what I was doing now?* If so, and since I was there snooping, I decided to snoop a little more. Don't ask me why or what I was looking for; I have never felt William would be the type to cheat or that I would find him on an Ashley Madison–type website seeking to meet another adulterous partner.

Then I found *it*, a folder in his documents file with my name on it. Right there in plain sight. I hesitated, a little afraid to discover what was in the folder. I paused briefly and then double-clicked the folder. One small, solitary image was staring back at me. I could see that it appeared to be a pornographic image. I double-clicked the image to enlarge it, and there it was: the couple we'd seen in the video way back when. How had he gotten the image, a screenshot? I guess it wouldn't be that hard.

Then I noticed something else. I'd been busy looking at this woman's hips and legs opening wide for his huge cock. Then I saw the beautiful brunette's face…or lack of it. William had replaced her face with a photo of mine, and it was clearly a very amateurish Photoshop job.

At first, my blood boiled in a knee-jerk reaction. *How dare he?* As I thought about it a little more, I wondered if he was using this photo to masturbate. I knew I had been avoiding sex and that we hadn't been as

41

amorous as William would have liked. I knew he must be masturbating to satisfy his needs. My anger meter drifted down from hot to warm.

Now what? Do I take this newfound information and confront my beloved? Do I confess to snooping? I was perplexed because I felt I had violated his privacy in a way. Okay, so maybe more than just in a way. Do married couples have a right to privacy? To keep secrets? To a private fantasy? I don't know exactly what impulse caused me to snoop, but it seemed like William and I were growing apart and not together. I know; I probably should have brought up my questions to William and just asked him directly what he was doing on the computer. I should have asked him to share it with me. Now it seemed I was compounding a problem I had initiated by avoiding sex. I wanted to blame William for all this, but as my anger settled down, it annoyed me that I had to accept my part in it.

The more I looked at the picture on William's laptop, the more I found myself getting turned on. It wasn't long before I was touching myself, having my orgasm with the thought that it was me in the photo.

Not long after my euphoric endorphin rush, guilt started to make its way into my psyche. *How could I let myself get so turned by this thought of having sex—taboo sex, interracial sex—with another man?*

When we would watch porn together, I was usually more turned on by the woman than by the man, but even then, I never fantasized about another woman. On those times when William would talk about how turned on he was, he spoke about his fantasy of me having sex with another man. What turned me on was how aroused William was by this fantasy.

I stared at the picture for a moment longer. *Could I?* I tried to imagine what was going through her head. What was she feeling physically and, most importantly, emotionally? Then I clicked out of the folder and closed the computer. And then I did something, and to this day I don't know why; maybe it was my comme il faut woman's intuition. I reopened William's laptop and entered the password once again. This time, I clicked on the e-mail icon on the desktop.

On the left-hand side of the screen was a column labeled Mailboxes, and below that were a list of e-mail accounts, WilliamTaylorESQ, WilliamandRebecca, and JumpEarlyQuickly. The first was William's work e-mail; the second, our joint e-mail; and the last was an e-mail we both used when we had to sign up for something and provide an e-mail address. It was a sort of junk e-mail address.

I had access to the last two and reviewed them at least daily, so I ignored those two. I hovered the cursor over WilliamTaylorESQ and hesitated. Guiltily, I looked over my shoulder, half expecting to see William standing there.

My hand trembled on the mouse. Had our marriage come to this? I considered our marriage to be the exception. We were the perfect couple, weren't we? We were open, honest, and had no secrets, yet here I was suspiciously snooping on my husband. *Suspicious of what?* I wondered. *Was it more out of guilt? A reflection of my brooding?* Up until recently, I had never kept sex from William. I was almost always accommodating when he initiated our lovemaking. Often, it seemed the more we made love, the more I wanted sex. Now the flip side was the less often we had sex, the less often I wanted it. I found myself initiating sex more often than William. I was the one who initiated sex now, not William. I remembered him saying, "I want you all the time. I'm afraid to ask because I'm afraid it will be too much for you." But here I was, and for the past few months, I was doing what I loathed in other women. I saw it as a destructive tool used in a dysfunctional marriage. Here I was throwing my own little pity party and passive-aggressively withholding sex from my husband.

I hesitated, took my hand off the trackpad, and started to get up. But then I double-clicked the trackpad, the cursor still over the WilliamTaylorESQ e-mail link. I opened up William's work e-mail. On the left was a long list of e-mails with their subject line. On the right-hand side of the screen was an e-mail from a client thanking William for the great work he had done for his company.

I scanned down the list of e-mails. Mostly they were from other members of the firm, and in the subject line were cases or names of clients. Out of boredom, I opened a few. Many of them were asking for William's opinion. One was from John, asking William if he had time to play golf with some prospective clients. I opened the Sent e-mail folder and found more of the same, most of which were William giving his opinion on certain cases. There was part of me that felt ashamed. Not only had I not trusted my husband, but I was a voyeuristic, Peeping Tom, jealous-crazy wife.

And the more I thought about it, the more I internalized my guilt. I knew deep down inside that William was right: I *was* very turned on thinking about the interracial scene. There was a secret part of me that wanted to be that free, like the woman in the video. I enjoyed sex…a lot.

By the time I clicked on the Deleted folder, quickly scanning those e-mails, I just felt worse about myself. I noticed a button: Restore Recently Deleted E-mails. *I had come this far; I may as well continue down the snooping wife's rabbit hole.* So I went ahead and clicked on it. Again there was not much there.

Then I noticed one e-mail in particular. *What I was secretly looking for?* Maybe I didn't feel so ashamed of myself. It was an e-mail from Stacey Donovan. I vaguely remembered William mentioning her name. I double-clicked the e-mail icon. *I think she was someone new to the firm. Wasn't she the Harvard grad?* I thought.

> *William,*
> *Thank you for your kindness. I appreciate the lunch and that you took the time to drive me around town to show me the different areas of my new city—okay, this is a damn big place. The traffic is going to take some serious getting used to...sorry, I am running on, I agree Pacific Palisades is probably the place for me. I agree with the Mayberry feel, and the place has some intriguing charm to it. I wonder though as a single woman if I will feel out of place there. It seems like there are mostly families living in this secluded bastion of paradise. Thanks again for lunch at Café Vida. I can't believe I saw Angelina Jolie on one of my first ventures out, and she is so gorgeous; it is intimidating.*
> *Stacey*

My blood boiled. I didn't remember William mentioning this escapade. I clicked on the web-browser icon and then to the home page of William's firm's website, clicked on the icon for Newsroom, and scrolled down to the announcement of a new partner, Stacey Donovan. I hovered on the hyperlink and then clicked on the blue underlined name of Stacey Donovan.

First I noticed the picture of a stunning redhead. *My God, this woman is beautiful!* I thought. Then I read some of the highlights from her bio. Stacey Donavan graduated summa cum laude from Harvard Law School, where she was the managing editor of the *Harvard Law Review*. She also served as clerk for Chief Justice John Roberts.

The résumé went on, listing accolade upon fucking accolade. All my insecurities came rushing up front and center stage. Jealousy hung

44

around my neck like a millstone, followed by a pang of fear and hurt. *Could I lose William? Was I failing as a wife? Did William blame me for wanting to leave the church?* So many thoughts swirled about in my head.

A Fork in the Road

Sometimes you choose the fork in the road, and sometimes that fork chooses you. Life happens, perpetually propelling us forward. You can't stop it any more than you can stop a massive wave.

That night, William was in our bed, tired from his one-day trip to San Francisco, reading his book, *The Art of Fielding* by Chad Harbach. There was a part of me that wondered, *Had my husband been gone on this trip with this new coworker?* My stomach churned, and I was getting ill thinking about it.

Something instinctively told me either I fight for my husband and end my self-imposed pity party right here and now or risk losing him. I like sex—no, I must admit: I *love* sex with my husband. I have to let go of my fears and accept that the thought of being with someone different did excite me. The photos on William's laptop did arouse a desire within me. I was going to hold nothing back tonight. I decided I wasn't going to admit to my snooping earlier today. Instead, I would quiz William. Besides, I was still horny from looking at the photos on his laptop. I made my way to the bathroom and came out in a white outfit—thigh-high nylons, black pumps, a garter belt, and a frilly lace bra. I walked over to our bedroom door and locked it.

William looked up from his book. "Oh my, what have we here?" he asked.

I smiled and licked my lips. "I need you," I purred.

"Wait. Not to ruin the moment, but have I forgotten something? Our anniversary? Father's Day? Valentine's Day?"

"No, silly. Just shut up and put that book away before I hurt you with it."

All through foreplay and then during our lovemaking, the image on William's computer kept slipping into my mind, stirring an undercurrent of emotions.

I waited, wondering if tonight William would bring up his fantasy. Then, in the throes of our lovemaking, he finally did. "Baby, I get so turned on thinking about you having sex with the guy in that video."

"The black hunk?" I asked, even though I knew the answer.

"Yes, it's so hot."

I had never fully participated in William's fantasies. By not "fully participating," I mean I just let him talk. Sometimes I would think

46

about the woman, but other times I would drift off into my fantasy of something more sublime, but tonight would be different.

"What would you want me to do to him?" I asked.

"Get on your knees and suck his big cock." William moaned more than spoke the words.

"It would be so big and would barely fit in my mouth," I purred.

"Oh God, you'd look over at me."

"Yes. I'd be worried you'd be jealous—or worse. That it would somehow change our relationship."

"No, baby, I'd be so turned on," he reaffirmed.

"Would you be turned on to know I can taste his precum?"

"Oh yes, I would."

"He'd be so hard now. I can feel him in the back of my throat," I added for William's visual imagination.

"Oh God, baby, I'm going to come."

William stiffened and groaned. I touched myself, releasing my orgasm.

Paper or Plastic

"Ma'am, would you prefer paper or plastic?"

"Oh." I was startled out of my thoughts of wondering how many times in my lifetime I had been to the grocery store. "Paper, please." I turned to the bagboy. His eyes were not on my face or my groceries. *Was he looking at my breasts?*

He looked up, a little embarrassed. I made a mental note of the name on his badge: Kurt. I smiled as I tried to hide my irritation.

"You got it. Paper," Kurt said.

I gazed at Kurt for another second. *He's cute enough,* I thought. Tall, blond, broad shoulders. A surfer, I surmised. *Was he checking me out?*

"Would you like some help with your bags?"

Usually I would say no. I surprised myself as I answered, "That would be great."

"Anything else?" Denise, the cashier in her midfifties, asked me with a knowing smile.

"Um, no. Thanks," I answered nervously.

"Awesome day," Kurt said, looking up at the sky as we walked to my car.

I had been more than a little nervous, because back in the store, there was something about this twentysomething kid checking me out that aroused me. "Yes, it is, Kurt."

"I wish I was at the beach," he confessed.

"Yes, that would be a good place to be." As I spoke, an image played in my mind of Kurt in his board shorts, dripping wet, his broad shoulders and six-pack abs glistening in the sun as he taught me how to surf.

We continued with our small talk all the way to my car. I watched Kurt as he loaded my groceries into the back of my car. *Does he find me attractive?* Through the years, other men had made comments when I was out without William. Kurt was a younger, college-age kid. I couldn't help but wonder if I still had it and if Kurt was interested in me. *Was he actually flirting with me, or am I letting my imagination get the best of me?* He'd been ogling my breasts, after all. Of that, I was pretty sure.

Clumsily, I tried giving Kurt a twenty-dollar bill as a tip.

"Sorry, ma'am, I can't take a tip."

"Rebecca."

"Huh?" he spluttered with a half smile that would melt the heart of a woman at any age.

"My name is Rebecca, not Ma'am," I said, smiling.

Kurt extended his hand. "Kurt, but I guess you already know that." He pointed to his name badge and smiled. He had not only a seductive smile that left me weak but also beautiful baby-blue eyes.

His hand felt strong and—different—in my hand. I blushed, feeling a sense of guilt. I had brought Kurt out to my car because thinking that he found me attractive had aroused me.

I had never acted on anything like that before. I was curious, and now my imagination ran away like a team of wild horses. *What would it be like to be with Kurt and his strong, broad shoulders and surfer's physique?* I found myself wondering. *Could I do it? Could I have sex with Kurt, someone who aroused something so forbidden in me?* For so many reasons, I wanted to say no; still, there was no denying I was turned on by the thought. My body reacted to the beat of its own drummer. I was wet.

A New Fantasy

That night, when William and I made love, he was talking about me with the black man in the video, while I was thinking about the surfer bagging my groceries—Kurt, his broad shoulders, washboard stomach, and tight ass.

I felt a certain amount of guilt. In a way, it felt like cheating. I was thinking about someone other than my husband. It didn't stop me from coming, thinking about the taboo of being with another man, especially a younger man like Kurt.

It seemed as if I were crossing a bridge to a land I had never been to before, a land where sex was just sex. Not love, no emotional ties. Just sex.

Was I liberating myself? Trying to justify my withholding sex from William or trying to sanitize some deviant carnal behavior? Can a woman think about sex in a transactional sense as a man can—or is it demeaning? I knew I was overanalyzing everything; it was all new to me, and after all, isn't that what writers do? Scrutinize every word, every scene, every motive, and every emotion? Besides, it was part of my training as a lawyer, and after all, William and I were expanding our way of thinking.

Was Kurt objectifying me when he stared at my breasts? Was I objectifying Kurt when I fantasized about him while making love with my husband? Is my husband objectifying me when he is making love to me and fantasizing about me with another man?

All the questions, feelings, and thoughts made my head spin. *Finally*, I thought, *we are human, after all. We have physical needs and wants, and so many things can give us pleasure.*

After all, what makes something wrong in our eyes? Who defines wrong? Should we feel guilt just because the society says so, even though we are not hurting anyone? Besides, a few thousand years ago, there wasn't a notion of so-called love. It was just chattel and lust. Women were virtually sold into marriage. Thus the question asked in traditional marriage ceremonies: "Who gives this woman?"

Perhaps the translation should have been, "Who trades this woman for a dowry?"

A woman was no more than property to be sold and bartered. Is a woman more than a being without rights, someone to do chores, a fertile field for a man to plant his seed, bear children, and provide pleasure for her man? Why can't we be in touch with our physical yearnings? Because I'm a woman, do I have to deny them still? I couldn't help but think of all the women in Utah on antidepressants. Was it in part because they were denying themselves carnal pleasures for whatever their own personal reasons may have been?

A Random Encounter

I don't often go to the Third Street Promenade, the outdoor mall in Santa Monica, but on this occasion, I was in a store waiting in line. The African American businessperson in front of me, who was wearing a very expensive, well-tailored suit, turned around and smiled. I noticed his eyes; they seemed intelligent and kind. He had movie-star kind of looks.

On my way home, I wondered, *Of all the men I'd noticed at the Promenade, could I have slept with any of them?* I never really thought of strangers in that way before now. It seemed foreign and not necessarily appealing. I decided that the next time William and I made love, I would mention the black man I met while waiting in line.

Later that night, William was in bed reviewing some work he had to submit the next day. I came out of the bathroom dressed in a black teddy. "Hey, soldier, you in the mood for some fun?"

"Oh baby! You're spoiling me. I could get used to this."

I climbed into bed and kissed William. He moaned. Usually he was the one who kissed me. I reached down and took his cock in my hand. With a few strokes, he was already hard. I very quickly made my way down and started giving William a very sloppy blowjob.

"Oh God," he groaned.

"You taste good, baby," I said, taking his cock out of my mouth and licking the head. "This black guy flirted with me in line at the store." I exaggerated, knowing my husband would get so aroused. "I think he wanted to fuck me." With that image in both our minds, I put William's cock back in my mouth.

In the heat of our foreplay, the talk about sex with someone else was making me hot and wet. I wanted William's hard cock buried deep inside of me.

"You better stop. I'm going to come," William said while pushing my head away and at the same time trying to pull me up.

A Simple Recipe

Laura was a friend of mine who worked with her husband at their financial-planning firm. We had lunch at a little café in Santa Monica. The one irritating trait about Laura is that she loves to gossip. This time, Laura brought up a friend of ours, Kim—well, Kim's husband, Dana, who had been having an affair with a younger woman.

"She's twenty years younger than Dana," Kim announced to anyone who would listen (and even to those who wouldn't).

During my conversations with Laura, I noticed that she loved to talk about an epidemic of men leaving their wives for younger women. Laura would always say, "It is so easy to keep your husband happy. It only takes a few minutes."

"What do you mean?" I asked.

"How many friends do we have who say they don't like sex anymore, especially Kim?"

It was true. Kim almost used to brag about it. "Dana would never leave me; I'd cut off his balls. I only have sex with him a couple of times a year, mostly on special occasions."

"Yeah, but—" I protested to Laura.

"No buts; just give a guy a blowjob once or twice a week. We all know a guy can't resist a good blowjob. Just look at President Clinton, Hugh Grant, and a host of others. I could go on and on, but then my food would get cold, and they might close the restaurant on us. Not to mention guys won't last that long; men climax so quickly, especially with a little bit of oral stimulation." Laura swore, pausing to take a bite of her salad.

"Oh God, your mouth is so good; you give the best blowjob," Laura moaned in a whisper, trying to be discreet, pumping a semiclosed fist close to her open mouth, simulating a blowjob and mocking men in general. "And you'll have the happiest guy in town," she promised.

She has a point, I acknowledged. *William never tired of blowjobs, and he never lasted very long.*

"Can I get you ladies anything else?" our handsome waiter asked. I noted that his skin looked like caramel candy, and his bluish-green eyes smiled at me a little longer than what you might expect from a waiter who had taken note of my wedding ring.

I felt a twinge of emotion. *Is this another guy finding me attractive—*

53

even...sexy?

"No, that will be it," Laura answered quickly, noticing the long connection between the handsome waiter and me.

"Okay, I'll be right back," he said. He smiled at me and held my gaze as he looked at my lips.

As our waiter walked away, I turned my attention back to Laura.

"Oh my God, he was totally hitting on you," Laura said with a schoolgirl-jealous tone in her voice.

"Come on, Laura, I'm at least twice his age," I said modestly as a warming sensation grew from head to toe and then gathered between my legs. "Now back to our prior conversation—is that what you do? Take care of your man?" I asked.

"Yep, and sometimes at work."

"What?" I said, shocked.

"Simple and quick." She smiled and winked. "And I guarantee he will never stray."

Another Random Encounter

As I kissed William, my hand was on his cock. "Are you fantasizing about me with a black guy?" I asked, knowing the answer.

"Oh God, that would be so hot," he moaned.

"At lunch with Laura, our waiter was checking me out," I teased.

"Oh baby, you're naughty."

"He reminded me of Denzel Washington."

"Was he into you?"

"Yes, and he was younger than us. He kept staring at my breasts," I whispered in William's ear.

"You are so beautiful, Rebecca; I am sure a lot of guys find you sexy and hot."

"I fantasized about taking his hand and leading him into a back room," I continued.

William moaned.

"Then getting on my knees and sucking his big black cock," I continued to tease.

"You're such a slut."

"Just the way you want me to be," I said in a hushed tone.

"Yes, I do."

"I would take his big black cock out of my mouth, and then he would bend me over and fill up my pussy with his massive cock."

"Oh baby" was all William could utter.

"I would feel his cock getting bigger as he's about to come. Then he would come in my wet pussy," I said, moaning.

Stroking harder did it; William came in my hand without warning.

"I'm sorry, baby," he said, embarrassed.

"That's okay," I stated with a wry smile, thinking about what Laura had said.

"What's gotten into you? That was so hot."

"You're welcome."

"Was your waiter actually checking you out today?" he asked curiously.

"Before I tell you, you need to go down on me, and if you're good, I will tell you all about it," I said huskily.

I am beginning to enjoy this, I thought.

Oh, to Wonder

As the weeks went by, whenever I was out and about, I would look at different men, wondering if I could have the kind of anonymous sex William and I talked about with a stranger. Very few men got my attention, and even fewer had any sex appeal. It became evident to me, based on just looking at men, that personality was more influential than a man's appearance. For the few with whom I did exchange more than a look and actually had a conversation, I found I was more open to the possibility. Maybe these men were more confident? The senses, smells, pheromones, the sound of a man's voice, and what comes out his mouth when he opens it were all a part of the spell they cast. *Does he seem intelligent?*

As I thought more about the question of anonymous sex, the question shifted from *Could I actually do it* to, more importantly, *Did I even want to?* What about the risks, especially the risk to our relationship? Was this just a fantasy between us, or did William really want this to happen? Did *I* want this to happen?

William would get turned on hearing about my adventures out cruising for men in the city. Then a funny thing happened: I was also getting turned on as I imagined what this man or that man would be like. Did I need a connection to have sex with a man? After all, men didn't (need a connection, that is). Was that why prostitution continued to thrive? Fast, easy, albeit transactional sex? How turned on was William going to be when I told him of my adventures? But first I had one more stop to make: the grocery store.

Wading Further In

As I approached the entrance to the grocery store, I nonchalantly checked my reflection in the mirror. I was wearing a short black tennis skirt and a low-cut blouse, with a push-up bra to maximize my sex appeal. The automatic door opened. Passing over the threshold, I casually glanced to see if Kurt was working. Sure enough, there he was, talking—or was he *flirting*—with a young, very attractive woman. I was surprised to realize that I was a little jealous. I tried to reassure myself that he probably flirted with most, if not all, women, but it was probably more the age factor that made me feel vulnerable.

I made my way through the aisles, picking up a few things along the way, including a case of Vitamin Water and two cases of plain old bottled water. These bulky items I probably could have waited for another week or so to buy, but asking Kurt for help out to my car with only a few items in my basket would only be too obvious. I headed to the checkout lines, specifically the one that would lead me smack dab into Kurt.

I found the one, and I made eye contact with Kurt. He smiled and waved before turning his attention back to his customer, an older woman, who looked over her shoulder at me. My bruised ego rehabilitated a little, knowing I was not completely over the hill yet.

"Good afternoon," Michelle the cashier said. *She was probably pretty in her younger days*, I thought.

"Good afternoon, Michelle. How is your day going?" I asked.

"Pretty good, thank you. How about yours?"

"Very well, excellent, splendid, and not good" was what I wanted to say to correct her, but I didn't. Instead, I turned my attention to Kurt. "How are you, Kurt? How has the surf been?"

"Overhead," he said, and I could tell he was searching his brain for my name.

Don't worry, Kurt, if you can't remember my name. All I want to do is see your mouth-watering smile and eyes and then later fantasize about you while I am having sex with my husband tonight. Even I was a little shocked at how quickly I allowed myself the freedom to let my imagination run wild. "Sounds exciting," I said.

"Do you need help out to your car?" Kurt offered, his blue eyes igniting my imagination.

Even though I am sure he made the offer to everyone, this made me feel better. It also inspired a crescendo of heat between my legs. "Kurt, that would be great."

Out at the car, I watched Kurt load my groceries and then bend over and pick up my case of water and then a case of soda. His broad shoulders, thin waist, and (I could only imagine) rippled stomach underneath his shirt and grocery-store smock captivated me. Once again I found myself wondering if I could go through with this. This was more than a fantasy. My knees felt weak as images swirled in my mind and what would it feel like to have this young hunk between my legs.

"Will that be all?" Kurt asked, his steamy blue eyes holding my gaze.

I so wanted to say, "No, I want to have sex with you," but kept it to myself, the lady that I am. "Yes, that will be it, Kurt," I said, disappointed and relieved at the same time.

That night, after going to the grocery store, I was fired up again. Being free seemed to be making me horny all the time.

Once again I delighted my husband, and in the midst of making love, I said, "This afternoon I met this hot young surfer guy."

William could just muster a moan.

"He works at the grocery store bagging groceries, helping MILFs out to their cars," I whispered.

"You wanted to fuck him?"

"Yes," I moaned, my orgasm building.

William groaned and buried his face into my shoulder. He pumped harder.

"I bet he has a young, hard, beautiful cock," I said, my arousal increasing.

William was coming hard.

"I bet he would make me come over and over again," I moaned. My orgasm left me satisfied and unfocused.

Curiosity

Several months passed by, and I would see Kurt occasionally at the grocery store. I always made sure I was wearing a seductive workout outfit or tennis outfit, something that showcased my legs and breasts. I would always make sure he took my groceries out to my car.

There were other men I had found when I was out running errands around town. Each time, I would tell William about them. We were having more sex than when we were newlyweds.

"William?" My head was on his chest. I could hear his heart beating.

"Yes?"

"Do you want this to happen?"

"Are you enjoying the fantasy?" he asked.

"I am," I answered, trying to hide my ravenous interest.

"What about during the day when you are out and you come across these men?" William asked.

"Yes, that also, but mostly it's the thought of how much satisfaction I know you get from it." I shamefully misrepresented the truth.

"Are you doing it just for me?"

"I think it may have started out like that," I answered innocently.

"And now?"

"It still is, especially knowing it turns you on, but like I said before, but I think I am past the stage where I'm just doing it because I know it turns you on. It turns me on too," I confessed.

"Knowing it turns you on turns me on even more. Knowing you are getting pleasure out of fantasizing about other men blows my mind," William replied.

"Let's just say—for the sake of this discussion—that I want to really live this out. Would you be mad if I said I think I could just have sex with someone? As long as you are there to share the experience with me?" I said thoughtfully.

"You've given this some thought," he said. The surprise was evident in his voice.

"I have, and I have a lot of questions."

"Curiosity killed the cat, you know," William replied.

"Exactly, but seriously, most importantly, would it change our relationship?"

"Yes and no."

I stared into William's eyes, searching.

"I think it would change to the extent that any experience changes a relationship. My hope is that it would make us closer," he added.

"Do you really think it would make us closer? I can't imagine being any closer than we are right now."

"I think it would," William offered.

"So are you saying you would be okay with it?"

"Under the right circumstances? Yes, I think I would."

I paused to consider William's response, thinking of Kurt and the black man in the video from years ago. William's hand was running through my hair, making me drowsy.

"So why do you think it would make us closer?" I queried.

"Sharing something so intimate and getting pleasure guilt-free is bound to bring us closer together. At least I would hope it would," he replied.

"Me, too," I whispered.

"Is that it?"

"No. You know me; there is always more. For starters, I am afraid you'd be jealous if I seemed to enjoy it too much," I said cautiously.

"You don't need to worry about that."

"What if he, the other guy, wants more?" I asked.

"You mean he falls in love with you or he tries to see you more?"

"Yes. I mean, we can control what we are thinking, feeling, and our rules, but now we involve someone else who may initially agree to the rules, but then things could change," I added.

"I've thought about that too," he said thoughtfully.

"You have?" I tried to sound sarcastically shocked, even though I was a little taken aback that William had also thought this through to this extent.

"I know I should apologize, but you know the way my mind works. I just keep drilling down, trying to see as many unintended consequences as possible and to see if they can be mitigated."

"Okay, Einstein, where did that amazing brain of yours lead you? How would this work?" I asked, getting turned on again.

"A local stranger or a stranger who occasionally comes to California."

"A stranger? Isn't that risky?"

60

"Yes, but I think there are ways of vetting them," he said.

"You *have* put a lot of thought into this."

"Yes, you're probably right."

"I'm glad you did," I said, giving my husband a soft kiss.

"I do have that conference in Las Vegas in September in four months. Maybe you should reconsider going with me," he said.

"You mean to meet someone there?" I asked hesitantly.

"It's far enough away from home. Who knows?"

"Hmm," I murmured. My head spun as I realized that I was getting horny just thinking about it.

Curiosity Leads to the Internet

After a week, I let William know I would go with him to his conference in Las Vegas. Before going, we thought we would sort of ease into or dance around these edges of this lifestyle. During this time, we had been on Las Vegas dating sites, searched adult ads for men looking for a hotwife or cuckold couple. *Hotwife* was a new term for me, and it described a committed couple who sexually shares the wife with other men. I was surprised so many couples engaged in this lifestyle. I suppose it shows how naïve we were. By looking under *male for hotwife* or *cuckold couple*, we figured there would be less explaining to do with someone who understood the lifestyle, and they would understand there would be rules and boundaries.

We searched through hundreds of profiles and ads. Some were well written and others not so much. As far as profile pictures…well, I think it is okay to mention I was over the dick profile pictures. Others were cute, with a sense of humor. Here are a few samples:

> *want ur girl to play with my big dick—m4mw*
> *i am young fit white dude looking for a chill couple to hang out with. first of all i am not bi just looking to play only with her. also i am std free and always use condoms. so what do u say we hang out and have fun im free today*

In his photo, he had a huge, uncircumcised cock sticking out of his jeans and an unmade bed in the background.

> *Big   Veggie   for   her—m4mw   (you   host)*
> *bbc male looking for a couple to have the wife sucking my cock…maybe more i am clean without drugs, diseases or hiv…recently tested…you be too send a picture and BBC4ME in the subject line Don't ask for pictures if you don't send.*

For his photo, he had a picture of his manhood next to a yellow squash.

> *30yr old bull, looking for casual fun M4WM, M4W—m4mw*
> *I'm 30 years old, 150lbs 5'10', straight, athletic, very good looking, Ivy League educated, respectful, kind, clean and dd free. Looking for local hotwives or visiting businesswomen for casual*

hotel fun. I'm okay with your man watching or joining the action, and I'm always happy to contribute to your photo/video library.

His photo showed a slim, in-shape torso without his prize possession. His ad piqued my interest. *Why would an Ivy League–educated man be on Craigslist?*

Massage for her while you watch—m4mw (Your Place) Visiting in town soon. Let's hook up NSA Massage while I'm here. Looking for a mature woman to be massaged and then satisfied by my huge 9 inch cock (27-50+) preferably. For mature woman who crave a relaxing massage and then a hard, young cock inside them making them cum! Disease free and clean, as I am too. Send me a pic of face or body (or both) back for fast response! Looking forward to hearing from you. Will voice verify or Skype to confirm.

His ad had two photos, one with a woman in bliss getting a massage and the other with him naked in front of a camera or laptop with his erection leaning to his left.

I just didn't seem to make a connection with the men in these profiles. None turned me on enough for me to say, "Yes, he is the one."

Curiosity Leads to Las Vegas

We arrived in Las Vegas early Friday afternoon. William's conference would start on Monday. I was a little nervous and excited to see what might happen. William asked if I wanted to go to a swingers' club, but I declined. I told him it seemed a bit much and too much pressure.

Our room was just not any room but a two-bedroom presidential suite on the top floor of a very swanky hotel.

We decided we would go out dancing Friday night, and if we had fun, we'd go again on Saturday night. The unofficial plan was for me to start taking a look around. Kind of like a kid in a candy store or maybe more like a kid in a toy store, where I could do more than just admire the candy from behind a glass barrier. I even planned to dance with a cute guy or two if it worked out.

On Friday evening, there was a very handsome man in his midthirties who got my attention. William went over and invited him to join us. He bought William and me a drink. We had found out his name was Mark, and he was here from Boston for a medical conference. He was a PhD, and his research was on stem-cell regenerative medicine.

He was interesting enough, and I danced a few slow dances with Mark. He rubbed up against me a couple of times. I knew I had aroused him because I could feel the heat of his erection against my thigh. The sensation of feeling another man's erection on my leg me made me feel uncomfortable at first, but the thought that I aroused him excited me. But I still wasn't ready. He wasn't the guy.

When we got back to our room, William and I had the most amazing sex. William told me how hot it was to watch me slow dance with Mark. I told him how I could feel Mark's cock against my thigh and how I thought about touching it. After a couple of mind-numbing, body-consuming, fire-breathing orgasms, we finally fell asleep.

Confrontation

On Saturday, we spent a good deal of the time at our cabana by the pool. The was no shortage of hunky guys showing off their muscles and ripped abs. The women were just as gorgeous, displaying the kinds of bodies enchanted by the springtime of life. I was definitely out of my league. These young women had lips, hips, perfect derrières, and breasts that must have cost them a fortune—or maybe it was just my enviousness and resentfulness toward Father Time's attacks. Somewhere beyond the soul of the music at the pool, I could hear the tick-tock of life, marking milestones.

At dinner we ordered a bottle of wine and filled the empty space with idle chatter, trivial conversation, and silence.

"Are you nervous?" William asked.

"About what?" I replied, even though I was pretty sure I knew what he was referring to.

"Tonight…and dancing?"

"Oh, that," I said, trying to sound as if I hadn't been thinking about dancing with other men. I was even excited to see what the night might bring. "No, not really. What about you?" I sort of lied. I wondered if I could really go through with having sex with another man. At the pool, there was plenty of eye candy, but in the flesh, none of them aroused enough carnal desire in me. Talking about it in the midst of our lovemaking and in the safety of my imagination was one thing, but here in the real world, it all seemed immeasurably different.

"I couldn't help but wonder if any of those guys at the pool piqued your interest," William said.

"There were so many young men, hunks with perfect bodies at the pool," I acknowledged, smiling.

"And did any of these so-called hunks interest you?"

I smiled and finished chewing my bite of salad. I took a sip of wine before I answered, "Not really. Honestly, I was more impressed by all the beautiful young women. In fact, I was rather intimidated by their gorgeous young bodies." This time I was telling the truth.

"Yes, but trust me, these guys have fantasies about being with a cougar!" William exclaimed.

At first I was hurt and then irritated. Was William calling me old? I would have expected him to offer something more like "You are more

65

beautiful than those young bimbos" or "Your body is just as gorgeous as theirs." But instead, he called me a cougar.

I placed my fork down and thought I'd give William another shot at redemption. "Do you really think those hot guys would be more interested in my weathered cougar body than those plastic Barbie doll bimbos?"

"I remember Stuart at the office mention that when he was younger, he was turned on by older women. And now that he is older, he is more interested in younger women."

I looked at my husband. *Not only have you dug a hole, you have proceeded to bury yourself.*

"Is that what you want? A younger bimbo?" I quipped as I thought about Ms. Summa Cum Laude, the gorgeous, redheaded new associate at his office.

"No, that's not it at all," William responded defensively.

"Not even a stunning redhead like Stacey Donovan?" I quipped as my anger boiled.

William put his fork down now, cocked his head, and narrowed his eyes. I could see the wheels in his mind working feverishly.

"I saw the e-mail," I added and took another gulp of my wine.

William sat back and looked skyward, as if begging for some divine intervention. I knew him well enough to know that he was still in shock and was trying desperately to put it all together. "Which e-mail?" he asked.

Seriously, is he digging a deeper hole? I wondered.

"Is there more than one?" I asked.

"Well, we work together, and she consults me on a few of her cases," he offered. *Was he trying to buy more time?*

"Have you ever traveled together?" I blurted out.

"What? No, never. Rebecca, I am confused. What is going on here?"

"The e-mail where she thanked you for driving her around Pacific Palisades and taking her to lunch. In our neighborhood, I might remind you."

I could see the look of confusion on his face as he tried to jog his memory. "Oh that," he finally said. He reached over the table and took my hand.

"Yes, *that*," I growled. "Normally that is something you would tell me about, maybe even ask me to be the gracious host and tour guide."

"That was a last-minute thing. Charlie was going to take her around, but he had to go to court unexpectedly."

"And you were able to clear your calendar at the last minute?"

"First of all, I didn't jump up and offer. Charlie sent out an e-mail, and I had a massage scheduled that afternoon. No one else had time, and I was going to go to my massage but decided to cancel," William explained.

Some of this sounded familiar. "So is that what you want? Someone younger?"

"No, not at all. In fact, I was going to tell you, but Miranda had a performance that night at school, you weren't feeling well, and if I remember, you didn't even make it to Miranda's performance. By the time we got home, you were in a Nyquil-induced coma, and frankly, it was such a nonevent, I forgot about it."

I recalled that night—my guilt at missing one of the kids' events, how sick I was, and how out of it I was for a few days. I did go to bed early.

"Rebecca, I don't want anyone else. I would never have an affair, and I am sorry I didn't tell you about it. You're right—I should have. Our marriage is everything to me," he admitted.

I felt a little off kilter, embarrassed because I had admitted to snooping. William never asked me why I was looking at his work e-mails.

"So you're not interested in a younger woman?" I asked.

"Unequivocally, not at all. And a younger woman is not our fantasy."

I took a sip of wine, my insecurities mellowing. "So do you really think one of those hunks would be interested in a little old cougar like me?"

"Baby, you are one hot woman. I see how men look at you. Those young bimbos have nothing on you," William insisted.

"Well, maybe they do have something more."

"I don't think so."

"More silicone," I offered.

We both laughed.

When we were back in our penthouse suite, I really wanted to have mad passionate make-up sex, but William was on a mission, and they would only hold our table at the club until ten thirty.

Introspection

That night, there were any number of bachelor and bachelorette parties at the club. William was right there with me, and there was no shortage of younger men wanting to dance with me. One of these younger handsome men, Gaylin from Salt Lake City, sat with us and had a few drinks. He sat so close to me our thighs were touching.

"Why aren't you dancing?" Gaylin asked William.

"I like watching," William said slyly as we exchanged a glance.

"That is so hot," Gaylin said.

"You think so?" I teased and put my hand on Gaylin's thigh. "You being from Salt Lake City and all," I drawled.

"Oh yeah, there is a lot of that going on in Utah," he admitted.

"What, in Utah, home of the Mormons?" William jested.

"You bet! There's a lot of wild things going on up there. I go to the gym, and I can't tell you how many married women flirt with me. Some have even asked me to go to their homes and have sex with them," Gaylin boasted.

"Wow" was all I could muster.

"Yeah, crazy, right? A few have even asked if it is okay if they can video the lovemaking. They say their husbands want to watch later."

"In *Utah*?" William uttered, shocked.

"Mostly Mormons."

I moved my hand on Gaylin's thigh and felt a massive hard lump underneath his jeans. Just then Gaylin lifted his butt off the bench seat. I initially thought he did that so I could stroke his hardening bulge, but instead, he pulled his phone out of his pocket and looked at the screen.

"Sorry, I need to take this—it's my wife," Gaylin said sheepishly, and like that, he was gone.

"I was just about to ask him up to the room," William admitted.

"I had my hand on his cock," I confessed; I could feel the heat between my legs, a heat that yearned for satisfaction.

"You did?" William asked, his eyes big as saucers.

"I did," I said and put my hand between William's legs.

"Oh my God," William said. "Well, we should wait for him to come back."

"I don't think so. I want this cock inside of me now," I demanded, giving William a squeeze.

Lying in our bed after an evening of dancing and torrid lovemaking that lasted through Saturday evening into Sunday morning, William asked, "Do you think we're getting cold feet?"

"Maybe I'm too picky," I said, letting out a nervous laugh.

"You picked me," he said with a grin, "so you can't be *that* picky."

Am I too picky? Or is it that, subconsciously, I don't really want to act out our fantasy? I had to admit that touching Gaylin's cock made me wet and horny. The whirlwind of emotions and thoughts seemed to paralyze me. It was one thing to fantasize about it with William while we were making love in the safety of our bedroom but quite another to act on it, yet I had inched ever closer to the proverbial fire.

Lightning Strikes

Monday and Tuesday passed pretty much uneventfully, except for the number of times we had sex. There was no sighting of Gaylin, unless you count the times William and I both shared our fantasies about Gaylin having sex with me.

On a crystal-clear, azure-skied Wednesday midmorning, I was lying out by the hotel pool, while William was in the last of his meetings. I heard a deep, booming voice. Out of curiosity, I looked up over the pages of the novel I was working on and saw this very tall, broad-shouldered black man walking and holding hands with a stunningly beautiful blond, blue-eyed white woman.

"How about over there?" he asked her, pointing to the lounge chairs next to the right of me.

"Sure, that's perfect," she said.

She was gorgeous. I felt a twinge of jealousy, and the sight of her hand in his hand seemed taboo. Then I noticed how large his hands were. He towered over her, making this beautiful woman look almost like a beautiful child.

"Excuse me, ma'am," the owner of the baritone voice said with a sexy French accent.

I looked up from my book and over my sunglasses, pretending not to have noticed the two earlier.

"Are these chairs taken?" he asked.

His eyes were kind and gentle. They were a beautiful mocha color, and they bored into my soul. I felt exposed, naked.

"No, they are all yours," I said, clearing my throat and smiling.

He returned my smile, and his eyes locked on mine. It seemed like the moment in those movies or television shows where everything around the main actors freezes and then the characters can walk around and do whatever they want to in the frozen ones. My heart was galloping as if reacting to some primordial instinct. I nervously broke eye contact and looked at his flawless companion and smiled.

"Thank you," they both said. They looked at each other and laughed.

I went back to my book. Out of the corner of my eye, I watched as he set down their pool bag. He pulled out a red-striped pool towel, the ones given out by the resort, and spread it over the chair next to me and said to her, "There you go."

"Thanks," she said as she took off her cover-up. She got some sunscreen out of the bag and began to smooth it on her body. Envious, and with jealousy, I discreetly examined this blond bombshell's body for some flaw, disfigurement, wart, maybe an abnormally humongous hairy mole. Let's face it—I was feeling my age, and my insecurity was rearing its ugly, petty head.

He took out another of the resort towels and spread it on the chair next to her but farther away from me. I have to admit I was a little relieved. I'm not exactly sure why, but I was.

I did notice they were both wearing wedding rings, so I assumed they were married to each other. I went back to rereading my book.

Soon my mind was drifting. It's funny that I noticed that the woman to the left of me was overweight and needed a makeover like they do on the morning shows. First, the woman appears with dated clothes and hairstyle and then magically she reappears, to the delight of the audience, a glamorous transformation of her former self.

The woman to my left had any number of flaws, yet I was not thinking her hips were too wide. She had cankles and cellulite, and her nose was too big, et cetera, et cetera. But this bewitchingly gorgeous blonde was to my right, and like a bird dog, I was trying to find even a minor blemish. Her breasts seemed perky and perfect, her tummy taut without a hint of an ounce of flab. Her hair was expertly styled, and her nails were immaculate. She was thin but not model or anorexic thin. She had a feminine but defined muscle tone.

She took off her sunglasses, and I saw she had the most attractive, exquisite blue eyes. *Talk about adding insult to injury*, I thought. Why does a god seem to take some people and dip them in a completely different DNA pool? Talk about making me feel inferior. Why did Mrs. Barbie Reincarnate have to descend from Mount Olympus—and sit next to me?

"Michael, dear, would you put some sunscreen on my back, please?" she begged in a seductive voice.

"Of course," Michael responded.

Now that she was facedown with her head in the crook of her arm and Michael was focused on the job at hand, I was finally able to get a good look at him. I was sure he didn't have any body fat on him, and my eyes explored his well-defined six-pack. His skin seemed as if it

71

stretched over muscle everywhere.

He poured some sunscreen onto his hands and then rubbed them together. His massive hands on her flawless body made this beautiful blonde look even more dainty. The contrast of his dark skin sensually applying sunscreen against her lighter skin brought back the memory of the movie William and I had watched so long ago. The man in the video was so well endowed, I couldn't help but wonder about Michael. *Does this man have the package to match his hands?*

While I was lost in my thoughts, he untied the straps to her top. Something about the gentleness of the way he untied her straps turned me on. Was it the idea of him undressing her? I looked at her hips and wondered what it must feel like to have someone like Michael between her legs—my legs. I was getting aroused. A wanting, a warmness yearned between my legs as my imagination wilted by the scene unfolding next to me.

"Would you like some?" she asked.

I assumed she was talking to her husband, Michael, but then I sensed that she was looking at me. She was not asking him, I realized. *The question was directed at me.*

"Oh…um…sorry. No, I think I'm okay," I replied weakly.

Had she caught me staring? Was I staring?

"Are you sure?" he asked, and his voice captivated my imagination. "It wouldn't be a problem. My hands are already covered in sunscreen," he added, holding up his hands to show me.

I looked at his hands. They were the size of large dinner plates. The girth of his fingers matched his hands. How would they feel on me? My thighs tensed; my thoughts ran wild. *How would he feel inside of me?* I thought shamelessly.

"No, I should be going in, out of the sun, anyway."

"We didn't mean to scare you away," Michael said.

"No, really, I think I've had enough sun for the day."

"If you change your mind," the buxom blonde said with a devilish smile, "and by the way, he gives a good massage too."

"Good to know," I said, blushing.

"My name is Trisha."

"I'm Rebecca. A pleasure to meet you."

"And I'm Michael," he said with a smile. His eyes gave off a sense of kindness.

"Very nice to meet you, Michael, and thank you for the generous offer."

I wanted to stay and feel Michael's hands on my body, but I felt like I had to leave *now*. His body was beautiful, as was hers. After four children and now in my midforties, I felt another trumpet of self-consciousness. I quickly put on my swim cover-up, gathered up my belongings, and whisked off up to our penthouse suite.

Voyeuristic and Alone

I walked over to the window in our room that offered a great view of the Las Vegas Strip and, more importantly, a view of the pool. Trisha and Michael were right where I had left them. I felt like a jealous schoolgirl voyeur. He looked like a giant from *Gulliver's Travels*. I marveled at his size, now even more pronounced from this view. *He must be or was an athlete*, I thought. What sport could he have played, I wondered. Basketball? Soccer?

William wouldn't be home for several more hours, and the yearning desire between my legs was reaching a feverish pitch. I decided to use our jetted tub and take a nice, relaxing bath. I turned the water on in the tub and waited for the temperature to feel hot enough to the touch, just so it almost scalded my hand. I took out some of my lavender essential oil and poured a few drops in the water.

While I was waiting for the tub to fill, I took a look in the wine fridge and found a bottle of sauvignon blanc that fit my fancy. I poured myself a glass of the chilled, amber-colored wine and gathered up the flameless candles that were artistically arranged in the suite. I placed a few of the candles on the bathtub and around the bathroom. I walked over to the balcony window and looked down. I felt like a schoolgirl with a crush. Michael had sparked my interest, arousing a primal need, one that demanded gratification.

I settled into my warm, cozy, scented bath. A sweet, warm mist caressed me, as did the pulsating jets. The faux candles provided the ambiance of some ancient sexual priestess rite. Relaxed, I let my imagination run free. As I rubbed my body with essential oil, my fingers soon enough found their way to my most erogenous zone.

I thought of Michael's huge hands spreading sunscreen on Trisha's white body. How intoxicating his hands must feel. I could feel my lips and clit swell. Inspired by the memory of Michael's warm and beautiful eyes, I wanted to make this last. I resisted the temptation to rush to an orgasm. Instead, I lightly brushed my swollen erogenous body parts. I continued to rub my inner thighs, my stomach, and my breasts. I gently squeezed my nipples and brought my breasts up to my mouth. I sucked on my nipples, being sure to give each breast equal attention. I let my tongue encircle each nipple and then flicked each one with the tip. I fantasized about Michael's hot tongue licking my lips and then my clit.

My left hand brought each nipple to my mouth as my right hand made its way down to my swollen lips. I spread my legs a little farther apart. I wanted him inside of me. I wanted him to fill me.

I continued to let my imagination run wild, and I fantasized that Michael's large, masculine hand was caressing me. I moaned as the thought sent shivers through my body. My hand applied more pressure to my labia. I did not want to put direct pressure on my clitoris; it was much too sensitive for direct pressure. I slowly spread my lips and inserted one finger and then two, all the time fantasizing about the touch from my imaginary lover. I became obsessed by the thought of Michael touching me, inserting his finger into me. I moaned again. It was as if my body had a mind of its own, and with a scant warning, all of my carnal desires unleashed. My orgasm exploded, sending pleasurable bolts of lightning rippling through my body. Tremors rippled through me. I let out more than a moan as I raised my hips and now pressed three fingers deep into my wet vagina. The image and thought of Michael between my legs and inside of me brought me to my second orgasm. As the tension left my body, replaced with the endorphin high from multiple orgasms, I kept my eyes closed, tried to catch my breath, and relaxed back in the water.

A postorgasm shudder rippled through my body, leaving me trembling, and then a wave of guilt and shame tried to make its way into my psyche. "William is okay with me having fantasies about other men. It is his fantasy, too," I whispered to the shadows on the wall from the flickering candles. "He wants to watch me pleasured by another man."

Three-Door Puzzle

I heard the electronic lock on our hotel room disengage. I looked up from my laptop and the novel I was working on. I had become so engaged in my characters' lives I had lost track of time.

"How is the great white hunter?" I asked.

William set the room keycard down on the desk and then his briefcase. "Bored to tears and hungry as hell."

"I'm sorry," I said. *If he only knew about my day*, I thought. I had to hold back; I didn't want to spring it on him all at once.

"How was my fair maiden's day?"

"Interesting, to say the least," I teased.

"Oh really? Did you get much done on your novel?"

The events of that morning and my fun time in the bath had energized me. "I did, actually," I answered honestly.

"Oh, that is great. But I am as hungry as a bear, and I would like you to hurry your cute little butt up so we can go get some dinner."

"We could order room service," I offered, raising my eyebrows. Even though Michael had ignited a fantasy flame of desire, I wanted William. I craved sex with my husband and yearned to tell him about Michael during our lovemaking, knowing the retelling of my adventure at the pool would drive William mad with lust.

"You've been cooped up all day, and so have I—in that boring conference room," William added.

"If you say so, Captain."

"Indeed I do. Now get your scallywag butt in gear," William said in his best pirate voice.

As I was getting ready, I was mildly surprised at how turned on and nervous I was. It was as if this secret me was set free from the inner chamber of some medieval castle. After all, had not society and the Mormon Church been judge, jury, and dungeon guard? At the moment, an epiphany sauntered in from some deep crevice in my mind: *No, I had been judge, jury, and dungeon master.* I locked this erotic part of me away in some remote cell within my psyche. I made myself a prisoner, never to see the light of day but to believe the shadows on the wall are my reality. This afternoon, I had released myself from my self-imposed shackles, if for only one moment.

How do you tell your husband you were so turned on by another man that you came home and masturbated and had multiple orgasms thinking about having sex with this Adonis of a stranger? Or was it more? Was I ready? *Could I actually do this?* Most importantly, how would William react? I kept going back to these questions, but my relationship with William was more important to me than the air that I breathed.

Admittedly, the only times that we had ever talked about me having sex with another man was when we were making love, watching erotic movies, or after sex. That conversation was never part of what I would call our normal lives as husband, wife, father, mother, lawyer, writer, PTA parents, soccer coach, or basketball coach. It was kind of our secret life or fantasy life. Even though I brought up men I had shared an innocent moment with, it wasn't until I was safe in our home, our room, with my husband that I let the fantasy out of the proverbial bag. I was sure no one would ever guess this fantasy of ours was what we talked about in our lovemaking.

So when to bring it up? At dinner? On the way to dinner? After dinner? Or should I wait until we were making love?

Out Loud

We sat at the dinner table, surrounded by the resonance of the busy restaurant, lost in our thoughts. I poked at the pink salmon on my plate, while William sipped his Pinot Noir.

"William?" I said. Unsure if I wanted to bring up what had transpired at the pool and then afterward in the bathtub, I continued to surgically separate the tender pink salmon on my plate. My beautiful, wonderful, loving husband looked at me, smiled, and put down his glass.

"Dessert? Did you take a peek at the menu?" he asked, thinking he had read my mind.

"No, but now that you bring up the subject—"
We both laughed. I loved when he laughed. It brought out a certain childlike sparkle in his eyes.

"My steak is so tender; you really should have a small bite," he said.

"Well, my salmon is fit for a king," I countered.

"So what's for dessert?" he asked.

I finally said in a rush, "How much do you like our fantasy?" It had started out as *his* fantasy, but over time, it had become mine too. And now I guess you could say it was *our* fantasy.

"You know how hot it gets me," he answered.

"Okay," I said softly.

"It's getting me rather aroused right now, thinking about it. Why do you ask?" His eyes were piercing, searching.

"I like it also."

"But? What is it, Rebecca?" he asked as he reached across the table and took hold of my hand. "Are you okay?"

I was searching my soul, afraid of opening Pandora's box. I still struggled with the question. *Is this really something I want to take from fantasy to reality?* Moving our fantasy from the safety of our most intimate moments seemed like such a big leap, even though we had moved so far down the road already.

"I guess I want to know for sure. Is this more than a fantasy for you? Is this something you actually want to fulfill?" I asked, my voice trailing off. "You watching me having sex with another man?" I knew I was crossing some hallowed and imperceptible threshold.

William tilted his head and narrowed his eyes. I loved this man and would never want to do anything to hurt him. A prick of resentment flared up again as I thought of Stacie Donovan, the beautiful redhead William had taken to Pacific Palisades. *Would he ever do anything to hurt me?* We had discussed the events of that day, so why was it rearing its ugly head again?

"I know it's complicated, but, yes, I do. Like I think I have said before, I believe it is more important that *you* want to do this. I believe it would be a mistake if the only reason you, we, would do this is to please me," William said.

We both sat in silence for a moment.

"Let's just suppose I was okay with it," I said. What I wanted to rehash now was Stacey.

"Suppose?"

"Yes, I want to walk through it." I reluctantly decided that I was going to let my fixation on this beautiful young redhead go—for now.

"Do you think you're having second thoughts? Because I'm a little bewildered. Isn't this the reason you came with me on this trip, so you could go down this path, explore, and see if you found someone who sparked your interest?"

"I know, and you're right. I am more than just a little nervous…because I think I may have met this someone," I confessed.

"Wow. What? Really?"

"Yes," I whispered.

William set his fork down and took a big drink of his wine. "Okay. So do you want to tell me about him and how, when, where?" His voice trailed off as he looked around.

I could sense William was trying to temper his excitement and at the same time was exercising his patience with me. I felt as if I was meandering into an ice-cold pool.

"But first, let's suppose I *want* to do this. Are you okay with whomever I choose?" I asked, searching my husband's eyes.

"Yes. He is your choice."

"Okay, but what if we get into it and I chicken out or you get jealous?" I asked and then realized I was laying the preliminary foundation for my question about Stacey.

"I suppose that could happen, but I don't think I would get jealous. Most importantly, if you change your mind, then by all means, it's over; I mean, we stop."

"I think I asked this before—" I started to say.

"No, I'm not gay," William interjected before I could finish.

We both laughed at this.

"No, that wasn't my question. Are you doing this because you want to have sex with someone else? I just want to know," I tried to say reassuringly.

I wasn't sure my decision to rehash Stacey Donovan was born out of guilt because of what had transpired at the pool and then the pleasure I got fantasizing about Michael.

"No, not at all! I have no interest in someone else. I would get pleasure from watching you unleashing a carnal side of you."

"So not even with a cute associate at work?" I wanted to take it back as soon as I asked it.

William held my gaze, studying me. I could see the wheels turning in his head.

"Well, you know—" I stammered, trying to recover. "Stacey *is* gorgeous and smart." I tried to smile over my fear William would leave me for someone else.

My eyes stung, and I resisted bringing my napkin up to my eyes for fear that I would start crying and make a scene here in the restaurant. It seemed odd; I was about to tell William I was ready to live out our fantasy, yet I was afraid William wanted someone else. Wanted someone—specifically, Stacey—in ways that transcended just the sexual. My unfounded fear was that he was out of love with me and in love with someone else, someone younger and beautiful.

William reached over and took my hand. "Rebecca, I love you and would never hurt you. Not with an associate, not with a partner, not with a client, not with a movie star, and not with anyone."

I felt embarrassed for snooping, but at the same time, I was still bothered why William hadn't told me about his afternoon with Stacey. Then I realized I hadn't completely shared everything about my time in the tub after my encounter with Michael and Trisha.

This was a moment of truth. Did I want to have sex with Michael because I was afraid of losing my husband or because I wanted to emancipate some carnal part of myself and have an intimate experience with another man? As my mind flashed to Michael, my body responded with a hotness deep inside. This *was* something I wanted.

"I need and want only you, but at the same time, you want to watch me have sex with someone else. It's confusing," I babbled further.

"I can see your point, and it is a logical presumption, but my—our—fantasy is different than what you might be thinking."

I looked down at my fork in silence, wondering what to say next. I debated whether or not I should admit and apologize to my prying into William's laptop and e-mail. Somehow I realized he knew. After all, hadn't he left the mocked-up photo on his laptop for me to see?

I decided to drop it.

"Well—" I paused, wondering how to put this, because it seemed like such a leap and next big step. "I saw a guy at the pool today."

"Oh wow," William said, genuinely surprised.

I expected William to say more, but he was still undoubtedly surprised by my unexpected revelation, and I was sure he was trying to process how I had just shifted gears.

"But he is with his wife," I added.

"That complicates matters," William said, and we both laughed.

"She's blond and flawlessly beautiful, and he's handsome, one of the biggest men I have ever seen. He must play sports, I think. Maybe soccer or basketball." I was babbling.

"Not football?"

"I think he's French, because he has an accent."

"And so all men with French accents play soccer?" We laughed again.

"I must admit I am perplexed about how this would work, since he is here with his wife," William stated.

"Maybe I just want to say it out loud, especially about someone who probably isn't attainable."

"Yeah, I'm not sure how we would even start that conversation. 'Excuse me, but my wife would like to bleep your husband,'" William teased.

We both laughed. That made me feel better.

"You're right. How would we broach the subject?" I asked.

"Without me getting punched? You did say he was a large man," he added, raising his eyebrows.

"Yes, he is; I would say nine-tenths of a giant," I insisted with a scary grin.

"Obviously, if he were here alone, it would be different. I must admit, you telling me out loud that someone sparked your interest is a big step. So thank you for sharing, and now let me think about your mystery man and his wife."

Ta-Da

"Is there anything else I can get you?" our waiter asked.

Then, right on cue, Michael and Trisha sat down at a table just behind and to the left of William.

"Rebecca, do you want anything else?" William asked me.

"Um, no, I'm fine, thank you," I said nervously, smiling at our waiter.

"Take your time," the waiter said, setting the bill down on our table.

"They're right over there," I whispered with a slight pointing gesture to William's left.

"What? Who?" William asked, instinctively looking over his left shoulder.

Apparently, he was not trained in the art of being a sleuth CIA operative. Michael and Trisha noticed William looking, and then they smiled and waved.

He turned his attention back to me. "Wow! She is beautiful. And he is a big, handsome man," he said, emphasizing *big*.

"What do you think?"

"You mean living out our fantasy with this couple? Or did you mean dessert?"

"You're a smartass," I hissed as I stole a glimpse at Michael.

"I'm still processing everything, but if you're sure...I'm game," William said.

While William was adding his two cents, Michael caught me red-handed peering. He smiled and nodded. Michael's actions caused Trisha to turn around.

"What should we do?" I asked. Trisha waved to me. I shyly returned her wave.

"Did one of them just wave to you?" William asked.

I nodded. "She did," I said, a little shaky.

"While I pay the bill, why don't you get up, stop by their table, say hello, and offer some small talk?"

"Really? Is that not too obvious?"

"No, just pretend you're on your way to the ladies' room."

"William, I am so nervous."

"You'll be okay."

82

A Moment of Truth

As I stood, my heart thumped wildly. *Just be natural*, I told myself, but there was nothing natural about what I was going to do.

"Hello. How was the pool?" I asked.

"The pool was fantastic," Trisha responded.

"Yeah, I hope we didn't scare you away," Michael added.

"Oh no, not at all. My skin can't take much sun, and I wanted to get back up to the room and have a relaxing bath before my husband finished with his meeting," I said as I pointed to William. As a glance passed between them, my discomfort grew.

"Well, enjoy your dinner. I had the Alaskan salmon, and it was wonderful," I offered.

"We're going to be in the hot tub later if you and your husband want to join us," Trisha said as I was about to walk away.

"Thanks. I'll talk to my husband, and hopefully we'll see you out there," I said, almost biting my lip. We nodded and waved our good-byes. I was a little woozy with excitement as I made my way to the exit. I waited outside the restaurant for William for what seemed like an eternity.

"What took you so long?" I asked, grabbing his hand.

"They stopped me and introduced themselves!" William exclaimed.

"They, meaning *they*?"

"Yes, they," William said, laughing. "And they have names, Michael and Trisha."

"You know their names?"

"Yes, and they invited us to join them later in the hot tub."

"What? That was *my* big news!" I announced. I was a little disappointed I didn't get to surprise William.

"I think they were afraid they were too forward."

"Why would they think that?"

"They mentioned something about you running off every time they show up," he said, smiling.

"Really?" I asked, embarrassed.

"Yes, not to mention I almost laughed when Trisha said they were afraid they were too forward, inviting us to the hot tub."

"Why did you almost laugh?"

"Well, when we announce to them you want to have sex with her

83

husband—"

We both chuckled. It did seem funny but also absurd. Butterflies of self-doubt were giving me a feeling of stage fright. Could I shed my inhibitions and generations of indoctrination that said that sex is bad and dirty, that a woman must be monogamous and pure, that sex happens only in marriage and is sacred? I also wrestled with the church's teachings, ingrained in our psyche, about the taboo of interracial sexual relations. These seeds of doubt tried to creep into my mind, but I knew I had moved past them.

Back in our room, I shakily changed into my bathing suit. As I was brushing my hair, William walked up behind me and pressed against me. He rubbed his hands on my hips while kissing my neck. I was so turned on already; I thought I might have an orgasm just from my husband's touch. William's hands felt very good against my body. It felt as if my whole body would burst into flames. His hands moved from my hips down my thighs and then back up, tracing my sides until he cupped my breasts. I was very wet; I *wanted* William. I pressed my butt against his groin and could feel the hardness of his erection. I turned around and kissed him full on the lips.

"I want you," I said as I wrapped my right leg around his. I was grinding my pelvis against his erection.

"I want you too, baby," he said.

I started to untie the strings on his board shorts when he stopped me.

"No, let's wait and see what happens."

"Are you kidding me? I need you inside of me now!" I pleaded.

"It will be better afterward, no matter what happens."

Angel Wings

As we walked toward the large hot tub at one end of the pool enclosure, I noticed the silhouette of two heads. My heart started to flutter with excitement, but then to my disappointment, I quickly realized the two silhouettes in the mist were another couple.

"Looks like they're not here yet," I groaned, trying to hide my blighted hope.

"Well, it's to be expected, I think. They hadn't even ordered when we left," William said.

"I know, but you know me—Ms. Patience." The curiosity of what the night would bring was making me very nervous and excited.

We put our towels down on a chair and kicked off our flip-flops. William shed his T-shirt, and I slid out of my pool robe. As we climbed into the hot tub, the other couple, probably in their late twenties, got out.

"I hope we didn't scare you away," William said to the couple.

"No," the man said, "we have an early flight tomorrow."

"Well, have a safe trip," William added.

"Thanks. Enjoy the beautiful evening. The water is perfect," the young blond woman said.

"We will," I replied.

As she turned around, I noticed a beautiful tattoo of angel wings that nearly filled her whole back.

"Oh, this feels so good!" William exclaimed, sinking his body into the warm turbulence of the tub.

"Do you think I should get one?" I asked William, pointing to her tattoo.

He looked and then turned back to me. "That's an amazing tattoo, but you know you already have beautiful angel wings."

"Ah, you're so sweet," I gushed and kissed him.

"Do you think they'll show up?" I asked as I put a leg over his thigh. "After all, they are the ones who invited us." I strategically rubbed my leg against William.

"I think they will, but that is still a long way from any of this happening," he said, pulling me close to him. "Just the thought of *it* is making me so hot."

We kissed for some time. I was so horny I was ready to do William

85

right there in the hot tub in front of the stars, the entire universe, and anyone else who cared to watch.

"Sorry, we didn't mean to interrupt," a familiar baritone voice said in a hushed tone.

Lost in the moment with my husband, the hot tub, and the romantic ambiance, I was startled. Then I was embarrassed as I waited for them to say "get a room" or more appropriately "go to your room." It's funny how the brain works and processes so quickly as I recognized the voice.

His voice.

William broke away first. "Oh, sorry, we got carried away," he said.

"It's okay; we can come back later," Trisha chimed in.

"No, I'm sorry…romantic night away from the kids and all," I added clumsily.

"We hope you don't mind, but we brought a couple of bottles of wine," Michael said, holding them up.

"Oh wow, great," William responded.

I sat in the hot tub in silence. I was so nervous about what might occur that I was afraid my teeth would chatter. It seemed as if some mystical fairy godmother had turned me mute. I was staring at Michael's muscular thighs and then his rounded and well-defined rear end as he set the bottles of wine on a nearby patio table. Trisha dropped her robe on a pool chair. I desperately looked for some flaw in her body, but I was too entranced by Michael to let my jealousy take over and pay too much attention to her gorgeous body.

"Oh, this feels so sweet," Trisha said as she sank into the swirling, foaming waters of the hot tub.

"I hope you don't mind a red blend," Michael said as he handed us each a plastic cup.

He took off his shirt; the ripped abs had not been an illusion of some earlier dimension. His sexy body was just as I had remembered it. I was curious, but I tried not to stare at his loose-fitting board shorts as he stepped into the hot tub and sat down next to Trisha. I remembered asking William if all black men were hung, and he had said, "No, not all, but when they are, they are *hung*." Michael put his massive arm around Trisha, and my imagination ran wild. I imagined that she put her hand on his board shorts right where I had just been staring. William pulled me closer, saving me from my runaway, almost obsessive, thoughts.

86

"Such a perfect evening," William said, breaking the silence.

"Indeed," Michael said.

"So Michael and Trisha, what brings you to wonderful Las Vegas?" William asked, because it was probably obvious to everyone the cat had my tongue.

"Vacation," Trisha responded.

"Yes, a much-needed vacation. And what about you two?" Michael asked.

"I am here for a conference, and Rebecca is doing a little writing," William said.

"An author?" Michael asked.

I nodded; the cat still had my tongue.

"What genre do you write?" Trisha asked.

"Mostly historical fiction," I finally responded.

"Anything we might have read?" Michael asked.

"Probably not," I said.

"She's just being modest," William interjected.

"A humble writer? I didn't know there was such a thing," Michael teased.

"I suppose it depends on the genre. In my experience, most writers of fiction are introverts. Writers of self-help books? Now that's a horse of a different color. To quote the great Wizard of Oz," I said and laughed nervously. *Wait*, I thought in a panic. *Who said that quote? Was it the guard at the gate to Emerald City?* I couldn't remember, and I hoped they couldn't either.

"You're so cute," Trisha said.

I blushed, tongue tied. I could only take a sip of my wine.

"What about you, William? What is your conference for?" Michael asked.

"It's a legal summit," William said.

"Are you an attendee or a presenter?"

"Both."

"Impressive. So we're in the company of a legal celebrity," Michael declared to Trisha.

"Not really," William responded humbly.

"What area of law do you practice?" Trisha asked, ignoring Michael.

"Civil litigation."

"Now William is the modest one. He has argued cases in front of the Supreme Court," I interjected.

"Really?" Trisha asked. She looked at William a little more intently now.

Unannounced and like a rainstorm on a clear blue day, I was surprised when a wave of protective jealousy flushed my body. I had the feeling that Trisha *wanted* William. Their eyes locked on each other. *Trisha is so beautiful,* I thought. *What man wouldn't want her?* And then the thought of Stacey Donovan entered my mind front and center. The realization that my husband was handsome, successful, intelligent, and charming with a great sense of humor made me feel a bit uneasy and insecure.

"Interesting. Trisha is also a lawyer," Michael said.

"Really? What area of law do you practice?" William asked.

"Corporate M and A. Very boring stuff."

"Mergers and acquisitions…I think it's anything but boring, all those powerful egos you have to deal with," I said, trying to interject that I knew what *M and A* stood for and to quell my self-doubt.

"You're right about the egos of these pompous CEOs, but as tough as that can be, they are bright individuals who demand perfection."

"So how long have you been married?" Michael asked.

I was very grateful Michael had changed the subject. "Twenty-two years," I responded.

William nodded in agreement. "What about the two of you?"

Michael gave a short, controlled laugh. He looked at Trisha. "Dear, how long have we been married?"

"Long enough to take this trip," Trisha replied and grinned.

"A honeymoon?" I asked.

"No, not exactly," Trisha said.

William and I shared a glance.

"It's complicated," Michael announced.

"Really, how so?" William asked unabashedly.

"Are you easily offended?" Michael asked.

"No," I answered quickly.

"This seems interesting," William said and took a sip of his wine.

"I think this is going to require some more wine," Michael said as he got out of the hot tub.

I noticed that even his back muscles glistened as the water dripped down his back. His wet trunks hugged his round, muscular buttocks. It

88

almost seemed as if the Creator had taken a volleyball, inflated it, cut it in half, and placed it where most humans would have a rear end. I casually put my hand on William's cock, as everyone's attention was drawn to Michael. I had an image of the woman in the porn video, and then I glanced at Trisha and imagined her spreading her legs as her hands caressed Michael's muscular back.

As Michael turned around to refill our glasses of wine, I didn't have to wonder any longer. His wet shorts clung to his body, revealing the outline of his muscular thighs and more. Fortunately, I suppressed a gasp. William rubbed my neck almost like a trainer would rub his fighter's shoulders right before the first round of a fight. Michael caught me looking. He smiled an embarrassed smile, which made me feel a little better about my erotic curiosity. So quickly, after months of thinking I could be someone else, and in an instant, all that socially restrained, ladylike training came flooding back. I felt shackled by generations of puritanical how-tos—or, in this case, how *not* to behave.

"Okay, are you ready?" Michael asked, stepping back into the warm, swirling waters.

William and I nodded in eager anticipation.

"Trisha and I are not married to each other," Michael said and took a big drink from his cup of wine.

"A scandalous affair?" I asked.

"No," Trisha said as she shook her head and smiled.

Damn it, she is so beautiful, I thought.

"Do your spouses know?" William asked.

"It's more complicated than that," Michael answered.

"Hmm" was all I could muster as I timidly took a sip of wine.

"We belong to a group…a lifestyle vacation club," Trisha added.

"A swingers group?" I asked.

"Yes, but not in the traditional sense. Think of it as more of a swingers' vacation timeshare," Michael said.

"I'm a little confused," I responded.

"We are part of a worldwide group of couples who obviously don't look at marriage in a traditional sense. I hope that doesn't offend you," Michael added.

William and I looked at each other. I knew William was thinking they had no idea what we were thinking. I felt a little light-headed; the torturous yearning I felt was intensely fueled by the thought that this just might play out. Less than an hour before, this was just our fantasy, something to talk about while we were making love. Now it seemed there was a possibility this fantasy of ours was about to become our reality. A door was opening for us.

"No, this is fascinating. Keep going, please," William said.

"So, for example, my husband loves to hike and explore. Simply put, that is not my thing," Trisha said.

"My wife likes museums and historical sites," Michael continued.

"Michael and I just love relaxing, decompressing at the beach or by the pool. Our jobs are so stressful, a vacation filled up with a to-do list of activities is not much of a vacation," Trisha continued.

"That's more like work. When I'm on vacation, the last thing I want is a schedule to adhere to," Michael added.

"So are your respective spouses off with each other?" William asked.

"Yes, how does that work?" I asked, because now I was curious.

"To answer your question, no, but they could be. So each person fills out a profile of what they enjoy doing on vacation, along with a profile picture, information about themselves, pretty much the stuff you might find on a dating website," Michael said.

"As well as their interest in or, in some cases, disinterest in sex," Trisha added.

"Seems a little risky to jump on a plane to meet a complete stranger," I interjected.

"Yes, that's true, and I guess there's some trepidation initially, especially on the woman's part," Trisha commented.

"Is this your first time?" William asked.

"My third time," Michael responded.

"My fifth time," Trisha added.

"Any bad experiences?" I asked Trisha.

"Not for me," Michael responded and smiled at me.

His smile caught me off guard a little bit. I was so aroused thinking of being with this man. I imagined what his supple lips would feel like on mine.

"Each of my vacations has been unique, and I have had a gratifying time each adventure," Trisha added.

"Yes, the program is pretty amazing," Michael said.

"I'll say," Trisha interjected.

"How so?" William asked.

"What if your neighbor or coworker was on the site and they saw you?"

"That's part of the beauty of it. You can specify that you don't want to get any matches from someone local or who works at your company or even in the same industry," Michael said.

"Also, for me, it is how the program finds people you are attracted to that's so amazing. So the program gives you a hundred faces to look at, and you rate them. Then you're given about fifty different body types to rate. Then somehow, after it analyzes this information and matches you up with various possible partners, you go through and choose," Trisha said. Her excitement level seemed to increase with a certain sense of freedom from inhibition that made me a little jealous.

"It's fascinating how accurate it turns out to be," Michael added.

"What I am fascinated by—or maybe, more accurately, *surprised* by would be a better way to put it—is the fact there are so many couples who participate in this," William said.

"I know, right? But if you think about it, this is a worldwide organization, and if you look around at the multi-million-dollar properties, you might wonder if there are enough people who make enough money to afford these properties," Michael responded.

"I suppose that's true. I guess nothing should be that surprising. Still, I guess I'm a little naïve and astounded to learn that there are so many people interested in this kind of lifestyle," William said.

"I suppose so, but this is a network with many safeguards in place. There are a lot of people out there who are freeing themselves from the shackles of traditional monogamy. You'd be surprised," Trisha added.

"So when you're back home, do you participate in a swinger lifestyle?" I asked.

"Some do, some don't," Trisha admitted. "I don't."

"This is interesting," William said.

"You're not offended?" Michael asked.

"No, not me, but then, I'm not easily offended. I find human behavior and myriad choices fascinating," William replied.

"What about you?" Trisha asked me.

"I'm pretty open; sometimes it takes me a little longer than William to get there," I said.

"The program is pretty remarkable. There's a psychological exam administered by a psychiatrist, and the results are then reviewed by a team of psychiatrists, followed by an extensive medical test," Trisha said.

"And then there are the follow-up blood tests every six months, maybe more depending on your lifestyle," Michael said. "Obviously, it's not for everyone. There is the hefty application fee, five thousand dollars per couple."

"The application fee covers the cost of the psychological and medical exams," Trisha interrupted.

"Yes, and then there is the initial membership fee of one hundred thousand dollars and an annual fee of ten thousand dollars, which also covers the cost of exams. It's expensive, but it's all well run," Michael finished.

"That is expensive," I added. *You would have to be uberrich to afford that sort of club.*

"Why did you choose Las Vegas of all places?" William asked, not letting either Michael or Trisha respond to my comment.

I too wondered about that. If you have so much money, why not fly off to a remote island in Tahiti or Fiji?

"Just a quick getaway, with plenty to do. It's also so we can test the waters to see how we get along," Trisha commented.

"We've gone through a spiritual awakening of sorts. We've been turning over much of what we have been taught and looking at things differently and trying to have an open mind," William hinted.

"If you have any interest, we could give you a recommendation," Trisha said.

"A recommendation is the only way you can join, and it's the first step," Michael added.

"Interesting, but I'm not sure," William answered.

"Of course, you'd need to talk about it," Trisha inserted.

"I do have a question, though. Have either of you ever watched your spouse have sex with someone else?" I asked.

It was out in the open now.

"Not exactly," Trisha said. "Voyeurism isn't my thing. I think I like to participate too much. Now a threesome and a foursome, I have done. So that is why I say *not exactly*. My husband was in the bed next to me, but I was so focused on what I was doing I didn't notice, and most of the lights were off," she confessed.

"Did you like it?" I asked.

"It gets a little confusing and seems like there is a little choreography involved, so you can lose your focus and your orgasm." Trisha laughed. "Have you done anything like that?" she asked.

I could feel Michael's eyes on me. I reached for William's hand underneath the water and took a sip of wine with my other hand.

"Like a threesome?" I asked for clarification, even though we had only been with each other. I think I was just getting nervous.

"Or watching each other have sex with someone else?" Michael queried, smiling at me.

My imagination ran wild, and my body flushed with desire. "No," I finally said and looked at William. He smiled and mouthed *it's up to you*. "But we have fantasized about it." My voice quivered when I said those words.

This was one of those times when time seems to stand still. It was surreal to think that I had actually mentioned our fantasy out loud to someone else.

"Really? Now this is getting interesting," Trisha said with an inquisitive look on her face.

"We saw this video some time ago, and it got us both thinking and turned on," William commented.

"What was it?" Michael asked.

"It was a homemade video," I said.

"Amateur porn?" Trisha asked.

"Yes, it was a husband filming his wife having sex with another man," I added.

"A hotwife or cuckold," Trisha said. "And you were turned on?"

"What about it turned you on?" Michael asked before we could answer Trisha.

"Well, I guess at first it was just that it was amateur, so it felt sort of voyeuristic. And then the fact her husband was in the room watching and filming," William pointed out.

"I can see how that would be a turn-on, now that I think about it. It would be hot to have my husband watch me with another man," Trisha breathed.

"What about you, William?" Michael asked.

"I think I was initially turned on by the fact that a husband was sharing his wife, watching her get satisfaction from another man. It was something so taboo, but instead of jealousy, he was recording it for all the world to watch," William answered a little nervously.

"And she was free to enjoy sex with another man, to have an orgasm with another man. Yet, in an odd way, she was sharing it with her husband," I added.

"And it was a white woman with a black man," William said.

"Now this is getting even *more* interesting," Trisha commented.

"Maybe too much information and a little embarrassing," I admitted.

"No need to be embarrassed," Michael said to reassure me. I blushed a little at his effort.

"Yes, you're among like-minded friends. And well," Trisha said, "I'm sorry, but I must ask the obvious."

"Go ahead," William said.

I glanced at Michael, and he looked back at me and smiled. There was something in his eyes, a gentleness that made me feel safe.

"Have you ever lived out this fantasy?" Michael asked before Trisha could. He looked at me and then at William.

"No," I answered as my heart raced.

"So are you interested in doing this with Michael?" Trisha blurted out, sharing a glance with him.

William looked at me. I could feel all the blood rush out of my body. My heart was beating so loud I felt it might jump out of my chest. *This is it!* I thought. *The door is opening.* In that moment, we were invited through a threshold that would launch us into something unknown. I was a wife, a mother, a PTA president, and a daughter. Did that kind of person pass through this sort of door? My mind raced as it tried to make sense of everything I was feeling. *How would this change me? Us? Could I learn to live with myself? Was there any coming back or simply pressing forward? Would I be able to look my kids, parents, or friends in the eye? Would I be hiding something sinister? How would my answer change me?* For as quickly as the brain processes information, I thought in an incredibly short space of time how William might feel. Would he be disappointed? Jealous? Aroused? Relieved? But I quickly returned to the thought that this wasn't about William. *This is now about me.*

"I am, but, of course, it's not all up to me," I answered, surprising myself, looking from William to Michael.

Michael's smile turned serious as he looked at me. Now all eyes were on Michael. Ours seemed locked in some eternal moment of truth. Michael moved his gaze from me to William.

"William?" Michael asked.

"It's up to Rebecca, but, of course, I would want to be there," William answered.

"No pressure, Michael," Trisha teasingly said as she mounted

Michael, giving him a big kiss, and then dismounted. "He is off-the-charts well endowed," Trisha added. "You understand?"

"But, Michael, no pressure. Rebecca and I were laughing about this earlier today. How do you tell a couple that my wife finds your husband attractive and that she wants to have sex with him while I watch?" William said.

"Yes, a little awkward," Trisha said, laughing.

Michael looked at Trisha.

"Don't look at me for permission," Trisha said to him.

Trisha looked back at me. "You would be doing me a huge favor, Rebecca. Michael is so—"She held out her hands about two feet apart and raised her eyebrows for emphasis. "I am pretty sore, so I was planning on just giving him a thank-you hand- or blowjob tonight. Big is awesome, but too much is like eating a rich dessert as a meal all weekend long."

I looked at William and smiled. Michael looked at Trisha, put his hand on the back of her head, and brought her lips to his and gave her a long, sensual kiss. William had his hand on my thigh, stroking it. Then William kissed me. Both of us were lost in a lovers' embrace, lips locked, tongues exploring. We stopped. Then Michael looked at me and back at Trisha. "Are you sure?" he asked Trisha. The sincerity in his voice was reassuring.

"I am, Michael. I need to pack and get to bed. I need to be up at three thirty a.m. because my car will be here at quarter past four." She smiled.

My hand moved to William's groin; I was surprised at his arousal. Michael looked back at me. I was having trouble breathing, thinking he could see right through me. My initial reaction was to recoil from where my hand stroked, but I kept stroking. Michael smiled as he looked in the direction my hand was, and then he looked back at me.

Trisha took Michael's head in her hand and pulled him toward her. "I should start packing." When she kissed him, her arms draped around his massive, muscular shoulders. *What must that feel like?* Then, just as quickly as she had taken his head in her hand, she released him and was out of the hot tub. There was a momentary awkward silence as we all looked at each other while Trisha toweled off.

"Have fun," she said, smiling and waving.

We all returned her wave and said good-bye. In an instant, she was gone like some apparition.

95

We all said good-bye. Then there was some small talk among the three of us as the night grew darker and the steam from the hot tub rose toward the heavens.

"Should we go to our room?" William offered, breaking the silence.

Michael looked at me. "Are you sure?" he asked.

I was past the point of wondering. Michael broke our gaze and looked back at William. "Should I get some more wine?" he asked.

"We have plenty in our suite," William answered.

We got out of the hot tub and toweled off. For the first time, I was standing next to Michael, and I couldn't believe how tall and large he was. My heart was pounding, and my knees felt weak.

In the elevator back to our room, Michael and William exchanged small talk. I was left pretty much alone to my thoughts. I felt like I had agreed to go on a big, scary roller coaster, and now here I was in a line, ever so slowly inching toward the main attraction. And then a ripple that developed into a wave of insecurity washed over me as I thought of all the women Michael must have been with. *Would I be enough to please Michael? What about my four kids? How did giving birth to them affect my body? Would I be tight enough? Too stretched out?* Trisha's body was beautiful, flawless. Believe me, I checked her out like a mad scientist looking to discover some unobservable particle, hoping to find just one measly blemish in her, but I couldn't. Would my body turn him on? *He's here, isn't he? He must find me attractive, or I'm sure he would have figured out a way to remove himself from this fantasy of ours.*

As Michael held the elevator door open for us to exit, he shared a soft and genuine smile with me. I couldn't help but notice his large, muscular arms and his ever-so-masculine hands. As I exited, Michael touched my shoulder; his touch sent electric impulses through my body. I was tempted to turn around and do—what? I wasn't sure. Kiss him? Instead, I kept walking toward the door to our room.

Ground Rules

Once in our suite, we gravitated to the kitchen area. William opened the freezer and pulled out a bottle of Russian vodka.

"Shall we all take a shot?" William asked.

In the confined space of our room, Michael appeared even taller and larger than before. Being outside had given me a different perspective. William poured the vodka, and we raised our glasses. "To new friends and new experiences," William said.

With that, we drank. The chilled vodka both burned and warmed as it made its way to my stomach.

"Another?" William asked.

"Not for me," I said. I could already feel the effects of the alcohol and was already more relaxed.

"Only if you are," Michael said. "I can't let my new friend drink alone."

"One more, and then I'll open a bottle of wine," William said, pouring another shot into their glasses.

"Wait," I said. "I feel left out. So count me in." The alcohol had taken over.

We clinked glasses in a toast. "To a beautiful woman," Michael said, and he smiled again at me.

Those beautiful eyes. Does he want me as much as I want him? I was wet already, and I thought my body would burst into flames soon.

We set our glasses down on the counter. As William took out a bottle of red wine from the wine fridge and got the wine opener, he said to Michael, "So there are a few ground rules."

"Of course," Michael said as he lightly stroked my arm.

His touch sent a second round of excitement through my body. I looked at his muscles and noted that he was defined everywhere. It looked as if God had taken a thin sheet of skin and stretched it over the most beautiful body ever.

"First, Rebecca is in control, and if she changes her mind at any point, that's it," William said, studying Michael.

"Absolutely," Michael agreed.

"Second, nothing rough or abusive—verbal or physical," William continued.

"Not my thing at all. My preference is slow and easy. More akin to

97

making sensual, sweet love, Barry White style," he said, rubbing my back.

As I stood next to this gentle giant of a man, his touch was so arousing I thought I was going to explode right then and there.

"The way this will work is you will sit next to each other on the couch. We have a glass of wine. Once we finish our first glass of wine, I will get up to refill our wineglasses, and then, if Rebecca wants to proceed—and only then—she will initiate," William continued.

"That sounds well thought out and very clear. I appreciate it. Makes everything much easier," Michael said.

"Is that okay with you, honey?" William asked, looking at me.

Suddenly my throat felt as if it was dry and full of cotton. I nodded. "Yes, and on that note, I think I will head to the shower and rinse off."

I turned and headed to the bathroom. I could overhear William telling Michael that we had a second shower in our unit. He was welcome to use it to rinse off and to use the robe if he wanted to.

In the shower, I rinsed off and then washed my body quickly. As I ran my soapy hands over my aroused skin, I was looking at my body, my not-so-perky natural breasts, wondering if Michael would be turned on by the naked, natural me. I felt as if every erogenous zone in my body was swollen, engorged with blood. *No wonder men get so proud of their erections*, I thought. My entire pelvis felt aroused. It tingled with anticipation. I was afraid to pay too much attention to the sensations. With the warm water and my soapy hands, I just might have an orgasm right now.

Looking at my engorged breasts that Father Time, kids, and gravity had taken their toll on, I decided I would wear more than just my robe. I was a little surprised I was not having any second thoughts at this point. Instead, I was eager. The front of the line to the roller coaster loomed ever closer.

The warm water massaging my back, I became lost in thought, wondering what I was going to wear. Then I decided on my sexy black lace-and-mesh push-up baby doll outfit with matching V-string panties. No nylons. I thought William would be more turned on by the contrast of my white legs against Michael's milk-chocolate skin. The thought of spreading my legs for Michael sent shivers through my body. Finally, I decided to finish my attire with some black leather pointed-toe, pump high heels. I felt a small sense of panic. *How long have I been in the shower? Have I lost track of time? Did Michael leave, thinking I've changed my mind?*

98

I turned the water off and quickly dried myself. With the towel wrapped around me, I stepped out into our bedroom. I was relieved to hear voices, including Michael's easily distinguishable resonant voice, in the other room. Their voices were muffled, so I couldn't make out what they were talking about, not because they were talking in hushed tones but because of the distance and walls between our room and the living room and the pounding in my chest.

Dressed for sex, I gave myself a quick check in the mirror. I felt sexy and confident about my look. I put my white robe on over my outfit and went to the chair to put on my pumps. I felt a brief moment of vulnerability as I heard their two masculine voices. *This is really happening.* It was just two men waiting for me and my intimate outfit.

I slipped on my shoes and stood up. I tightened the sash on my robe as I walked to the door. I turned the doorknob, took a deep breath, and then let it out. "Showtime," I said to myself and walked out of the bedroom, shoulders back, chin out, hips swaying, trying to muster all the confidence in the world.

As I did my best runway walk down the hallway of our suite, the clatter of my pumps on the hardwood floor announced my pending arrival. Both men grew silent. Both heads turned toward me. I felt like a bride walking down the aisle or an anticipated actress walking onstage. Then I almost laughed as I imagined myself a virgin, offered as a sacrifice. A willing virgin, I quickly added. Okay, not so virginal, but still willing.

Both men stood up as if on cue. Tossing my inhibition to the side, I opened my robe to give them a sneak peek.

"Wow," said William.

"You look beautiful," added Michael, lust in his eyes for me.

"So sexy," William added.

I quickly closed my robe and tied the sash. I took a seat next to Michael on the couch, with William seated to one side on the loveseat. The setting seemed surreal and a little unnatural—me next to another man, both of us in white robes like some religious ceremony, me in a sexy outfit underneath my robe and not next to my husband, who was in board shorts and a T-shirt.

Sitting next to Michael, knowing what was about to take place, I felt like a kid at Christmas. I wanted so badly to open my present. I wanted to gulp down my wine. I wanted to touch Michael. I wanted to open his robe and let my hands explore this beautiful man's body.

Being a lady, of course, I restrained myself. Still, I felt like a filly in the gate ready to race in the Kentucky Derby.

"My family moved from South Africa to France when I was two. My father was a diplomat," Michael said.

I had been lost in my thoughts and not paying much attention to the conversation; I was wondering what we were talking about.

"So you speak French?" I asked.

"*Oui, je parle le français. Tu semblez être la plus belle femme,*" Michael said in such a sexy French accent it enhanced my arousal. "Yes, I do. Dutch and German also," he added.

"That is wonderful," I said.

"And I went to college at Cambridge and graduate school at the Wharton School of Business at the University of Pennsylvania." Michael turned his attention back to William.

"An Ivy League man," William jested.

"Yes, sir."

William drank his last bit of wine. I looked at Michael's empty glass and then at mine. I was lost in thought. I still had about a quarter of a glass of wine left. William smiled at me as I took a drink.

"More wine?" he asked.

"Sure," Michael answered.

Knowing the meaning of all this, I suddenly I felt very nervous. My heart felt as if it was pounding so hard it would leap out of my chest. I could feel my hands trembling as I drank the last of my wine. I was now at the front of the roller-coaster line. I had to either step on the train or take the last-minute change-of-heart chicken exit.

A Paradox

"Yes, please," I said, offering my glass to William. *Oh God, this is going to happen!* I thought.

I was only able to hold William's gaze for a moment. Doubt and guilt swirled up like a dust devil appearing in the desert out of nowhere.

"Thank you," Michael said, handing his glass to William.

And like that, William was gone. I was alone with Michael. My thighs tingled as my arousal heightened. He turned toward me and smiled.

I was here now. *Is this happening?* Thoughts swirled in my head. With my trembling hands, I reached up and pulled Michael's face close to mine. I closed my eyes. Our lips touched, and I slowly parted my lips. I could feel his warm, minty breath as his lips slowly parted my lips even further. His warm, moist tongue entered my mouth gently and didn't move. The sensations of kissing another man aroused me to new heights. I so wanted just to mount him, but I waited. My tongue found his, and passion filled my entire essence. Every sensation was a new one, from the way the back of his head felt to his full, supple lips; his breath; and his tongue.

I wrapped my arms around his broad shoulders and kissed him deeply. Trying to get my arms around Michael felt like trying to hug a mountain. His body was muscle-hardened. I could feel the definition of the muscles in his arms, shoulders, and back flexing as he moved with my embrace and kiss.

We kissed passionately for a while—how long, I'm not exactly sure. I was lost in the new sensations when I realized I had not heard William softly set our wineglasses down on the coffee table.

Michael's hands, lost in my hair, gently held my head as we kissed. Heat and want spread through my body like an untamed wildfire. I waited for the sanity police to haul me away.

I have to have him and soon, my body screamed.

"You're so beautiful," Michael breathed between passionate kisses.

I pressed my lips harder against his and pulled Michael on top of me.

The weight of this stranger felt good. My hands explored his body. His muscles flexed as he moved.

How pallid and soporific this existence would be without mysteries.

I hesitated for a moment and then whispered in Michael's ear, "Shall we go to the bedroom?" I couldn't help myself; I wanted him *now.*

He kissed me again. "Sure, let's go," he whispered back.

We stood up. Seeing him, a man I would never see again, I knew I wanted to pleasure him like he'd never been made love to before. His body was long and lean, solid like a racehorse. He was built for sex. I wanted to see every inch of him, touch every part of him, lick him, suck him.

In the bedroom, I felt like a woman who has her cake and eat it too. I reached up to kiss Michael again. My hands opened his robe. I loved his chest; it was so hard and muscular. His nipples were erect, and I wanted to taste them. I circled them with my tongue. I ran my hand down his muscle-rippled abs. He pulled me closer; our bodies were almost perfectly aligned to feel every muscle movement. I could feel his excitement growing. How could I make this never end? I couldn't wait for him to pleasure me. I wanted this to be the fantasy beyond anything that Michael had ever imagined. I was more aggressive now than I could ever have imagined. I liked it. I liked being in charge. Michael liked it, too—I think! *But where was William?* Had he followed us into the bedroom? I wanted to find him, make sure he was okay, but I was selfishly focused on this man in front of me—the man I wanted to please, the man I wanted inside of me.

Then, surprising mostly myself, I untied Michael's robe and dropped to my knees. What I had seen earlier shrouded in the confines of his wet board shorts was now right in front of me. His cock was beautiful, like an irresistible, supersize milk-chocolate candy bar waiting to be devoured. The veins running from the base to the head of his cock gave the appearance of rivers crossing a continent, carrying the massive amounts of blood required to engorge his large manhood.

My hands slowly ran up and down his hard, muscular legs as I kissed his thighs, moving my hands to the inside of his legs…slowly. Crawling up this glorious body. His anticipation was growing. I could feel it. I could see it. I looked up into his beautiful eyes, and he was watching my every move. *Should I kiss his inner thighs? Yes.* He groaned. I didn't want to hurry. I could see and feel his hardness growing. He was huge. A moment of self-doubt crept in. *Was I experienced enough? Could I please him with my mouth? Could I even fit him in my mouth? What must William be thinking?* Again I wanted to look over, but I was completely focused on this man in front of me. Throwing my concern for my imperfect body to the wind, I allowed myself to feel sexy. I loved the way he lusted for me earlier when I teased them. In my passion, I untied my robe and let it fall to the ground.

I was going to move on. I continued my crawl upward. It was glorious. It was enormous. I wondered, *Will it fit inside me?* I was not sure I would be able to get him in my mouth. It felt like a solid rod growing. As my hands encircled its base, it felt soft, despite being so hard. The weight, more than the girth, almost made me gasp. I wanted to taste it. I kissed its head. I tasted his excitement. His body stiffened, and his murmur of pleasure told me he wanted more. Who was I to disagree? I wanted all of him. I held him firmly in my hands, moving them gently up and down. My tongue searched his tip and tickled the head. I tasted a bit of semen that had escaped. His slight hip movement told me he wanted more. I could feel his anticipation. I licked and sucked his head, slowly taking him into my mouth. Savoring his taste, my tongue licked him as we began to enjoy a slow rhythm together. He moaned. I wanted all of him. I opened my mouth as far as I could. It almost felt like my jaw was about to become unhinged in that moment. I wished I had the flexibility of a snake's jaw. Bobbing back and forth on his growing cock, I could feel it moving into my throat. There was so much of him that there was no place left for him to go. *Wait.* My tongue and mouth gently moved him into a position undiscovered before. He was still not all the way into my mouth. My left hand with my wedding ring on it stroked the base of his shaft. My right hand stroked what I couldn't fit in my mouth. I moved my right hand to his hard, round, muscled ass and pulled him toward me. He moaned with pleasure! He stayed, and I gently sucked him in unison with his long, slow thrusts. This was exquisite. He filled my mouth with pleasure. The back of my throat would be sore for sure.

"Oh, please stop," he begged. "You're going to make me come!"

I gave my jaw a rest as I pulled him out of my mouth. A trail of precum kept us connected. I licked up this string and then licked the head of his cock, both of my hands gently stroking his throbbing member.

"I want you to come in my mouth," I told him. Looking up at him, his hard cock pressing against the side of my face, I was lost in passion and an ecstasy I had never felt before.

He moaned. "Are you sure?"

I glanced over at William. I had never begged with so much passion for William to come in my mouth. I worried for a moment, but I was so hot with desire, I couldn't think. I just wanted what I wanted. I had tried before with William, and the taste? Let's just say I wish it were more like dark-chocolate ice cream. That is where our flavored condoms would come in handy, so on the rare occasions I wanted William to finish in my mouth, we would use the flavored condoms. Now this, with Michael, was different. *I* was different. I wanted to please Michael. I wanted to taste his cum.

"Yes," I told him, "just tell me in French when you are going to come," I begged.

"*Oui, madame,*" he said softly.

I put my new favorite toy back in my mouth. My jaw gently reminded me that I was only human. As my mouth and tongue enjoyed this new wonderful sensation, I looked up at this man, this man using my mouth for his pleasure. I felt something dripping down my leg and realized I was so turned on, my body was anticipating its turn.

He looked down at me, his eyes seemingly asking—no, *begging*—for permission to come. *Oh, please, yes,* my eyes responded.

His body was quickening its thrusts. "*Vous êtes si belle,*" he said.

My arousal level reached a magnitude I never knew existed. I worked my tongue, licking the underside of his shaft in my mouth in anticipation. His throbbing cock seemed to grow even bigger, hardening in anticipation, filling my mouth. I could feel his heart pounding through the veins of his cock on my tongue.

"*Je vais foutre,*" he said.

Then he stiffened, and his groan of pleasure was accompanied by a stream of warm, slightly salty cum. He exploded into my mouth, and his cum hit the back of my throat. I pushed his cock deeper into my mouth, taking in as much as I could. I swallowed, my hands still stroking and squeezing his shaft, feeling the reverberating pulses of the last remaining drops of his semen flowing out of his cock and down my throat.

I glimpsed over at my husband. I was so lost in the moment; I forgot he was here. His eyes were wide open. I was trying to read the expression on his face with the realization that I had another man's cock in my mouth. I continued stroking Michael now with both hands, drawing out every last drop. I looked at my husband and shrugged. He smiled.

Michael pulled me up. I felt his huge biceps, and then he plunged his tongue into my mouth.

My turn now? I wondered.

Michael pulled my black lace baby doll outfit over my head, as if he had done this a million times before. He gently dropped it on the floor. He cupped my breasts and kissed me with more passion. His tongue, mixed with the taste of his own semen on my tongue, added to my heightened state of arousal.

With Michael lying on the king-sized bed, it looked more like a twin or full. Moving my hands along his massive arms, my breasts pressed against his body, I breathed into his ear, nibbled on his earlobe, and brushed his lips against mine. His face was smooth. His large hand took my chin and moved my lips to his. His tongue explored mine. Softly, and then more urgently, his tongue sought deeper exploration of my mouth.

My hands wandered, rubbing and touching his lean, hard body. Images of a racehorse came to my mind, how their muscles seem to move and flex independently with no effort. I was sucking on his nipples as my hand made its way down to his cock. Even in a flaccid state, I was still surprised by his size, girth, and weight. I couldn't help but wonder what it would feel like inside me. I was worried now that it might hurt. I still wanted it, though.

I started to make my way down from his nipples, but he stopped me.

"Your turn," he whispered and reached down to remove my V-string panties.

"Do you want me to keep my shoes on?" I purred.

"You look so sexy in them," Michael sighed. "If you don't mind keeping them on," he begged.

There was something about being butt naked with a sexy pair of shoes on that made me feel very naughty.

My knees weakened as his arms surrounded my body and his lips brushed across mine. He was bringing me even closer as he tightened his viselike grip around my waist and lifted me onto one of his legs, so my wetness was sitting directly on top of his thigh. He teased me with his tongue as it tickled my lips and began a patient search of my mouth.

Did my moaning in anticipation please him, or was he secretly smiling at my body's stiffening and then melting into his in response to his pleasures? My hands were on their own mission. I couldn't control

105

where they were taking me. To his chest, the back of his neck, his head. Could he feel my nipples hardening? I accepted and gratefully responded to his tongue being everywhere—over my teeth, touching the roof of my mouth, plunging down into my throat. I sucked on his tongue. If only—my enjoyment of his sensuality was overpowering me to maintain any sense of control. His sucking of my lips, my tongue. He took my breath away.

With ease, Michael rolled me onto my back. Our lips and tongues locked in an untamed erotic embrace. My heart pounding, my mind felt as if aurora borealis were bursting in my head.

From my mouth, he moved to my ear, licking, probing, and sucking. Then, just below my ear on my neck, his lips sucked, and his tongue fluttered against my skin. I wanted to squirm; my neck was so sensitive. His hands were exploring my body. They seemed to be everywhere at once, my breasts, my hips, my back, and then on the back of my head. He kissed me again. His hand made its way down as his fingertips traced my body as he memorized every inch of me. I trembled as his hand made its way past my belly button. I instinctively spread my legs. His hand felt so large between my legs. His tongue found my tongue, and the two intertwined. My hips moved toward his hand. My body tensed as he kissed me deeply, his hand now between my legs. I spread my legs farther apart and moved my hips upward. Everything was so new and different—the way his body felt, his touch, his kisses, the back of his head, his hands, even his advances, if I could call them that. Over the years, I had become so accustomed to William, it was like playing the same songs over and over.

Then his fingers found their mark. He applied just enough pressure to my lips and clitoris. I pushed my pelvic bone against his hand and moved my hips up and down. My clit was very swollen and sensitive. I knew I should slow down, but my body seemed to have a mind of its own. A crescendo of pleasure was building, and I was quickly passing the point of no return. He slowly parted my labia as I moaned uncontrollably. Then he slid a finger right into my wet vagina at the same time the palm of his hand pressed against my clit. I groaned, moaned, and thrashed. I was over the edge. My body trembled as my hips took complete control. I started to come as he began kissing my neck. My hips were rocking back and forth, creating the pressure I needed against the palm of his hand. He plunged a second finger into my soaked vagina. I screamed out something unintelligible and collapsed down on the bed like a rag doll.

My body still trembling, I looked over at my husband sitting on a chair by the bed. I tried to read the look on his face. A part of me wanted to turn away in shame. Here I was—a good woman, a good wife, and for God's sake, a mother, daughter, and sister. I had just given a black man a blowjob and let him come in my mouth, all while my husband looked on. Now he had made me come. A certain tide of guilt rose up. Then William smiled and mouthed "I love you." My heart melted, and for now, the temptation to call it all off subsided. I was lying next to another man, and in spite of all that had just transpired, my husband not only wasn't jealous but also seemed to be aroused. There was no judgment, no ownership; I wasn't his. Instead of remorse or shame, an unexpected wave of freedom—from guilt, from religion, from expectations—filled my being. I seized the freedom to move forward, to experiment, and to experience joy guilt-free. I was no longer a wife, a mother, a daughter, and a sister. I was free—free from the shackles placed on me by expectations of others who felt the need to sit in judgment. Finally, I was free to be me.

I wanted to make my way down Michael's body and replace my hand with my mouth. I wanted him in my mouth so badly. I wanted him to use my mouth again for his pleasure. My throat was sore, yet it ached for more. Michael held me close, my body wrapped around his. My breasts were pressing against his chest. He kissed me slowly and hard, his tongue darting in and out of my mouth where I wanted his cock to be. The thought of his cock in my mouth was getting me aroused again. It was so big and beautiful and powerful.

I wanted him—no, I *needed* him—inside me. Michael kissed my neck as his hands explored my body, breasts, butt, and hips, first massaging and then stroking. The combination sent shivers through my body.

He moved from my neck to my shoulder and then down to my breasts. The warmth of his breath on my breast as his lips moved along a path and his tongue darting out now and then overwhelmed me. His hand cupped my breast, and he brought my nipple gently into his mouth. His tongue encircled my nipple, and then I was lost in the supple flickering of his tongue. He sucked on my nipple, his other hand around my waist as he pulled me closer to him. I could feel his cock on my knee and calf. I swear it felt as long as my tibia.

He had my breasts in each hand and shared time between the two, giving each equal attention. I wondered if he liked them or preferred bigger, gravity-defying ones like Trisha had.

His eyes met mine, and he smiled. "I love your breasts," he moaned as if he had read my mind.

"I think they like you, too."

His hands stayed on my breasts as his lips and tongue started their descent, kissing my abdomen and briefly licking my belly button. His hands released my breasts and slid behind my back; then they parted my thighs wider as Michael moved his body between my legs. He kissed my inner thighs. With his hands holding my legs apart for the first time, I noticed the contrast of his skin against my pale legs. I moaned, and my hips moved up as I spread my legs even farther apart.

Michael knew what I wanted, but he teased me, moving from one thigh to the next, his lips slightly brushing against my wetness. I let out another moan. He kissed my other thigh, while my hips continued to try to entice him, like a snake inducing some hypnotic state upon its prey.

Finally, after several passes, Michael stopped where my hips had been begging him to start. He kissed my labia, and his tongue parted my swollen lips. My body shuddered, and I grabbed his shoulders. I waited for him to go to my clit like William did; instead, he spent time licking the inside of my pussy and sucking on each labium.

"You taste so good," he whispered.

I could only moan as I pushed my clit against his tongue. The new sensations were driving me crazy. I moved my hips up and down, applying the pressure that I wanted, while Michael's tongue worked its magic. I moaned to let Michael know that I liked his tongue pressed against my clit as I moved my hips up and down. He understood my carnal language and gave me what I wanted. I could feel my second orgasm quickly building. My hips were moving faster and pressing harder against Michael's tongue.

I looked over at William. "I'm going to come," I said.

He smiled and mouthed "I love you" again.

As I started to groan, Michael slipped one finger and then two into my pussy, pushing them deep inside of me as I shuddered and convulsed in the most intense orgasm I'd ever had. I lost track of time and, for a second, felt like I might pass out. As my body started to relax, Michael let me adjust the pressure until finally I thought I could speak. "Come up here," I told him.

He kissed my pussy lips, pulled his long fingers out of my soaked vagina, and then replaced them with his tongue. I wanted to let out a scream something unintelligible, but I held back. He spread my legs farther apart, pushing them toward my shoulders at the same time so his tongue could go deep inside me. Then he licked me from the bottom of my lips to my clitoris and released my legs back onto the bed.

"Oh my God," I said.

"Did you like that?" Michael asked, grinning.

"Get up here," I said.

We kissed, and I could taste myself on his tongue and lips. I didn't know what possessed me because I'd never done this before, but I inserted Michael's fingers into my mouth, sucking on them as I looked into Michael's delicious, dark eyes. I licked and cleaned all of my juices off his fingers.

I loved the reserved sensuality of having my lips barely brushed by his. Was he being polite or just teasing me to see what I would do? Of course, I wanted more. Oh my—his tongue was exploring my mouth, my teeth, the roof of my mouth. I wanted to suck it down into my throat, to consume it, to have every bit of him inside me. My desire to have him be a part of me, within me, was frightening.

His mouth was sweet, and his tongue seemed endless, becoming firm as it sought to reach into my depths. I ran my fingers along his massive shoulders and enjoyed bringing him even closer to my tensed body. I thought I mustn't moan my delight at having him make me feel so very sexy, and I felt very naughty with my shoes still on. *Shall I suck on his lips, tease his tongue with mine?* Could he feel the hardness of my nipples straining against his body? I wanted more of him. I wanted him as close as he could possibly be. His arms were so powerful and tight around me they made me feel safe, protected.

His thigh between my legs reminded me of the passion awaiting me. I could feel his huge cock on my inner thigh. I wanted it inside of me. I wanted him to take me. To use me. To fill me and fuck me with his huge cock. I wanted to spread my legs and to please him. I needed to feel his body tense, and I want his cum inside of me. My reward.

His hands were exploring me as I tried to encourage him to get on top of me and enter me. The thought of it made me grind my hips into him. I reached down and took his cock in my hand. Even in a semihard state, the thickness aroused a slutty feeling of letting go. I stroked his cock a few times. I wanted him in my mouth again. I wanted to make him rock hard. I started to try to go down on him.

"No," he said and pulled me back up. "It's better this way."

I was a little confused. After all, what man turns down a blowjob? Without thinking, I looked at William. He only smiled and shrugged. I don't know what I was hoping. That somehow William might offer me an explanation? I also wondered if I had failed to give him a good enough blowjob before. Maybe I was unable to get my teeth out of the way of his massive, zucchini-size cock. He hadn't seemed to mind, and he had come pretty quickly.

"I want you to fuck me," I begged.

"Okay," he responded and started to get up.

Confused, I asked, "Where are you going?"

"To get a condom," Michael replied.

"You've been tested. Do I have anything to worry about?" I asked, hoping I knew the answer.

"No, nothing," Michael said, looking confused.

"I've only ever been with William," I told him.

The look of bewilderment on Michael's face changed to understanding.

"I want you inside of me," I breathed.

Michael looked over at William. "Is that okay with you?" he asked with his French accent.

"I've only ever been with Rebecca," William answered. "So it's up to Rebecca, and you, of course," he added.

Michael came back, his lips found mine, and he kissed me deeper and with more passion than before.

I spread my legs and pulled him into my kiss. I could feel his cock slide on my thigh. I tried to put his cock in me, and I had hold of it near the base, but it was so long and not hard enough yet that I clumsily struggled to try to accomplish my goal.

"Here, let me do this," he said.

I looked down and watched with insatiable curiosity as Michael took his cock and gripped it closer to the head. He squeezed, trapping the blood flow, engorging the head, making it even larger. He rubbed the head against my swollen pussy lips and aroused clit. I could see that with just a few brushlike strokes, the head of his cock was gleaming with the moisture from my pussy. I reached down and spread my lips. He pushed forward. There was a slight pain, and for a moment, I doubted he would fit, and then there was a pleasurable sensation like I had never felt before. He was inside me, filling me with a length and girth I had never known. I moaned and moved my hips toward him, trying to engulf his every inch. I started moving my hips a little too wildly, and he flopped out.

"I'm sorry," I said.

"You're pretty enthusiastic, but I like it," he whispered.

My French lover pushed inside again. This time, he didn't need my help; he was covered in my juices. He got on his side and kissed me and slowly moved his big cock in and out of me. I could feel him growing harder inside of me with every movement.

He got back on top of me, as my legs spread wide to accommodate him. I started moving my hips to meet his slow and gentle thrusts. In my eagerness to meet his thrusts, his cock hit my cervix right on the button, sending a short bolt of pain through my body. I let out a little yelp and froze up.

"Are you okay?" he asked.

"Yes, keep going," I said, moving my hips again.

He pushed himself up, and I looked at his beautiful body, muscles rippling, from his chest down to where we were connected. He slowly pulled his hard, glistening cock out of me. It was so big I was amazed that Michael fit inside of me and that he kept pulling further and further out. The sensation of the head of his cock leaving my pussy and then going back in was exhilarating. I was mesmerized as he did this a few times more. I could feel another orgasm building.

My hands were gripping his massive arms. I never knew someone could have such large triceps, and that only added to the sensation of his swelling cock inside of me, touching me in places I didn't know existed, places I knew had never been touched before. He moved his body down a little bit and at such an angle that his pelvic bone was stimulating my clit. I put my hand on his rock-hard ass and ground harder, pushing Michael deeper again. The massive head of his cock rubbed against my G-spot as he pulled out. I moaned louder, my body tense with pleasure, new senses exploding in my body.

"I want you to come," I begged Michael.

"Very soon," he said, smiling.

Then we kissed. His tongue was inside my mouth; I licked it, sucked it, and bit it. I was letting a part of me out, free to let go and only respond. After a momentary pause, I caught my breath.

Michael, with little effort, rolled me over on top of him and said, "I want you on top."

So in one swift motion, I was on top of Michael, and he was still in me. I propped myself up, extending my arms, first using the bed; then I put my hands on Michael's broad, muscular chest. I adjusted myself; the size and hardness of Michael were a reminder to adjust myself carefully. Ouch, there was a tinge of pain. There was nowhere else for Michael's cock to go. How was I going to do this? I wanted all of him inside of me but not this way. I couldn't sit straight up.

This beautiful man's hands were roaming my body. It was as if they were exploring me for the first time. I noticed again how masculine his hands were, especially on my body, and the contrast of his dark hands on my milky-white skin. I couldn't help but feel self-conscious as gravity pulled my breasts down. Michael cupped one and pulled me forward with his other hand. He was sucking on my breasts, and at this angle, I could move my hips up and down on his cock. I moaned, pulling his head into my breast. I wanted to fill his mouth the way he filled mine.

Michael was moving his hips. His cock was as deep inside me as it would go, pressing against unexplored areas of my pussy. The head of his cock seemed to fill me up. I was moaning louder, my clit was getting more stimulation, and I could feel another orgasm building. Before I knew it, my body tensed, and I let out a moan.

"Oh God, I'm coming again," I said.

My body trembled uncontrollably, convulsing and shuddering. I couldn't speak or open my eyes. Finally, I caught my breath. "Did you come?" I asked.

"Not yet," Michael said, smiling.

"Oh my God, you're going to kill me!" I exclaimed.

"Do you want me to come again?" Michael asked, reminding me he had already come once.

"I do," I said.

"Okay, any special request?" Michael asked.

"What?" I asked in befuddlement.

"Where do you want me to come?" Michael clarified.

"Yes, I want you to come in me."

"Okay, but how about a little doggy style first for William?" Michael offered.

"Okay," I said and lumbered off Michael, unsure of what he meant by "a little doggy style for William."

It took a lot of flexibility and some gymnastic moves because of the length of his cock. But I finally got on all fours. I had a brief moment of panic. I thought, *Oh please, no anal.* I would surely need medical attention after anal sex with Michael.

Michael adjusted our position so William would have a perfect view. Now I understood what Michael meant. From where William sat on a chair to the side of the bed, he did not have the best view of all the action. I looked at William, and his eyes were wide open. He was watching as Michael's enormous cock was about to enter my wet pussy. Michael separated my lips and advanced ever so slowly forward.

"Oh my God," I moaned.

"Wow," William said, still transfixed.

"Rebecca's pussy feels so good, William. Thank you," Michael said, moaning.

"You're welcome," William replied.

His hands on my hips, he pulled his cock out to the point I could feel the head stretching my pussy lips before going back in ever so slowly, to the point where he was up against my cervix. He stayed there and pressed past my cervix with the head of his cock. He stretched my pussy, and it was stimulating. Then he pulled out. I moaned with disappointment and moved my hips; I wanted all of Michael inside me again. We continued on a little while longer.

"Is this what you wanted, baby?" I asked William.

"Yes," William whispered.

"Is this as good as your fantasy?" I asked.

"Better," he admitted.

Michael continued to pump his cock in and out with long, exaggerated strokes as the head of his fat cock spread my lips open wide.

"Do you like watching Michael's big cock fuck me?" I asked.

"Oh God, baby, it is so hot," William responded. "Do you like it?"

"Yes," I breathed.

"I'm getting close," Michael said as he pulled out of me completely.

I rolled over and looked at Michael's gorgeous body and his huge cock pointing forward and upward, defying gravity and covered in my juices. I spread my legs wide and tilted my hips upward. Kneeling, Michael moved his cock forward and into my waiting pussy.

"Oh God, your cock feels so good. Come here," I said, motioning for Michael to lie on top of me.

Michael obliged me, and I grabbed on to his massive shoulders. Our hips were moving in unison.

"Use me," I begged.

"Oh God," he groaned.

"Come inside me," I said, moving my hips and trying to squeeze his cock.

Michael's body tensed. My arousal went through the roof as this good-looking man and his massive cock filled me up.

"Oh God, you're so tight."

I moved my hips faster. He tensed. He put his lips on mine, and his tongue pushed forward into my mouth.

"I'm coming," Michael announced.

His body was stiff. His cock swelled, if possible, even more. I moved my hips, rubbing the head of his cock with the back of my pussy and cervix. I could feel his hot cum spurt inside of me, and like a sudden, unannounced earthquake, I came again. I wrapped my legs around Michael, pulling him into me. I wanted all of him. Our bodies were trembling and convulsing together. Michael slowly pulled in and out of me, sending more shivers through my physically wasted body. My mind was in a euphoric state of mindless bliss.

We lay there for a while, Michael still inside of me as we kissed. Finally, Michael pulled out of me, leaving a void and coolness. I could feel the heat from my vagina against my leg. We lay in a lovers' embrace for a little while. We kissed softly. Michael's hands brushed over my body as if he was trying to commit it to memory.

"You have a beautiful body and spirit, Rebecca."

"Thank you, Adonis," I said, and we both laughed.

There was a part of me that wanted him to fuck me again, but I did feel physically wasted and yet totally satisfied. Bliss.

After a while, Michael asked William, "Do you mind if I rinse off really quick?"

"Not at all," William said.

"Thanks," Michael said. He gathered his clothes and walked to the bathroom.

"Come here," I said to William.

We kissed, and I felt through his board shorts his rock-hard erection.

"Oh baby, let me take care of you," I said while trying to pull his shorts down.

"Shouldn't we wait until Michael leaves?"

"No," I said as I put William's cock in my mouth.

I could taste William's precum. Not a lot different than Michael's. I made a mental note. *Do all men taste basically the same?* William was groaning and rock hard in no time, fucking my mouth. I didn't remember William ever being so hard and swollen.

"I'm going to come," William said.

I sucked and twirled my tongue with more energy, when William exploded in my mouth. I gagged for a minute—William was definitely aroused, I thought, as there seemed to be an endless stream of cum—before swallowing. I stroked William's cock, making sure I got everything out.

"Oh, sorry," I heard William say.

I thought he was talking to me because he had so much cum, but when I looked up, I saw William looking at Michael. I looked at Michael with William's cock still in my mouth. I kept sucking while looking at Michael. I got wet thinking about how much I wished Michael was behind me, fucking me while I sucked off William.

"Well done," Michael said and smiled.

William pulled his board shorts up quickly and then leaned over and shook Michael's hand.

"Thank you, Michael," William said.

"No, really, thank you, William." Then Michael turned to me. "And thank you most of all, Rebecca."

Naked and unashamed, I stood between my husband and Michael. I reached up and gave Michael a kiss. He didn't say no or recoil. I knew he could still taste William's cum in my mouth. His tongue explored my mouth briefly. We separated and said our last good-byes. Michael exited the room, and I heard the door close.

I took my husband's hand and looked into his eyes. "Thank you," I said. We kissed.

That night, after William had recovered, we made love with more passion than we ever had, even more than when we were newlyweds.

With William now fast asleep, I thought about what had happened that night and how far I had come. I had had sex with another man, a stranger, and my husband seemed to love me even more. There was no sense of jealousy or awkwardness, the emotions I was afraid an adventure like this might cause.

    I had, for the first time in my life, let myself go.

Uninhibited.

There was no going back.

www.ingramcontent.com/pod-product-compliance
Lightning Source LLC
Chambersburg PA
CBHW071323130626
46556CB00004B/1727